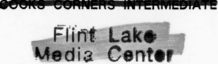

HARVEY
the
BEER CAN KING

HARVEY
the
BEER CAN KING

by Jamie Gilson

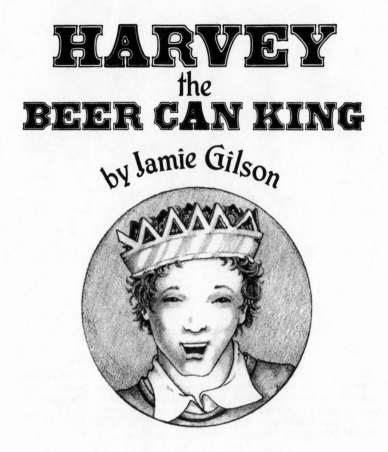

Illustrated by John Wallner

LOTHROP, LEE & SHEPARD BOOKS
NEW YORK

Library of Congress Cataloging in Publication Data

Gilson, Jamie.

Harvey, the beer can king.

SUMMARY: A twelve-year-old boy hopes his beer can collection will win him
the title of sixth-grade Superkid.

[1. Collectors and collecting—Fiction]
I. Wallner, John C. II. Title.
PZ7.G4385Har   [Fic]   78-1807   ISBN 0-688-02382-7

To Tom, Matthew and Anne—Superkids.

Contents

1 · Superkids

I used to like Quint Calkins, even though I hardly knew him. If you'd asked me which kid he was, I'd have told you he was the guy with the long black bangs, the kid who could curl his lip way up on one side like he smelled skunk. (I'm not saying that's bad. It's terrific. I'd do it myself if I could.) I knew he gave good birthday presents—stuff like monster models and plastic ice cubes with flies in them. He liked magic. He was better than anybody else at running the hundred. And that's about all I knew.

So when he told me one day in gym that he knew all about beer cans, I told him I had the best collection in town. Why be modest, right? And when he said his dad had just brought him two Pike's Peak Ales from Colorado, I asked him if he wanted to trade. "Sure," he said. "Why not?"

After school I bagged a few fairly choice cans and skateboarded down the hill to the park. Quint was already there. He was sitting on top of the high slide, holding a big brown grocery bag in his lap. And he was curling his lip at the line of little kids waiting behind him. Quint's a big guy, a lot taller than me, and those kindergarten kids couldn't budge him.

"Go away, insects. I *live* up here," Quint said,

leaning back on the line of them. "I'm king of this mountain." The kids on the slide stomped on the steps and shouted. This really little girl threw her big yellow beach ball at him. It almost hit his shoes. Quint sneered at her and started roaring down.

"Godzilla!" somebody on the slide steps shrieked. Quint turned on the group of them, whipping the sack around over his head. I could hear metal crashing inside.

"Hey, Quint," I yelled at him. "You got your cans in there?" I thought maybe I could stop a riot. Besides, I didn't want to trade for any beat-up cans.

He looked over, surprised to see me. "Naw," he said, really sarcastic. "I got a baby rattle, can't you see?" He shook his sack at the kid who'd thrown the ball. She kicked at it and missed. "I scare infants with it." He flung it up, grabbed it just before it hit the ground, and then tossed it over to me.

We sat on a grassy patch away from the slides and emptied our cans out among the dandelions. If Quint had a great collection he sure hadn't brought any of it with him. They were just cans like you'd find in park bushes after any old warm Saturday night. Only one was halfway decent. But I figured I might as well give the guy a chance.

"Quint," I told him. "This is your lucky day. You give me that Pike's Peak Ale and I'll trade you a Schlitz Malt, a Lone Star, and a seven-ounce Rolling Rock." I was *giving* them away. "OK?"

He flipped the hair out of his eyes and looked them over. When he found a scratch on the Rolling Rock, he looked up at me so I could see his lip arch in disgust. "Oh, why not?" he said finally.

"I'll tell you why I'm giving you three for one." I didn't want him to think I was a pushover. "They're doubles, that's why. And I've got to start cutting my collection." One of the kids from the slide ran by and stuck out her tongue. We ignored her.

"Cutting it?" he asked. "Why would you want to do that?"

I didn't *want* to, that's for sure. "Oh, my mom gave me the old Beer Can Lecture again this morning. The same old stuff about how she's put up with it long enough now and, Harvey Trumble, you get those smelly cans off the floor and into the trash. 'I mean it this time,' she said."

Quint dug a flat rusty Schlitz out of the bushes and arced it toward the trash barrel. It hit the edge and bounced in. Lucky. "Two points, star. Did she mean it?" he asked, as if he didn't care worth a rusty can whether she did or not.

"Probably not." She was always after me about them. But she's a pussycat. I lay back in the grass, resting the old head on the skateboard, rolling it back and forth to massage my brain muscles. "I'll tell her at supper that I've taken her advice and started trading down. That'll do it."

"Look, you really want to get rid of them?" Quint

11

asked, a little too quickly. "I'll take them off your hands for nothing."

You bet he would. He'd take them off my hands, put them in paper bags, and whip them around at little kids. "No thanks," I told him. "I'm just bluffing her. I won't trade down far."

I really like those cans. I think it's great how they come from Japan and New Jersey and all those little towns in Wisconsin and how they stack up in silver

towers in my room. I stretched out in the grass feeling good. "I like having more of them than anybody else. I wouldn't give them up for anything."

A bicycle skidded right in front of us and Suzanna Brooks, this whiz kid on wheels with the paper route, slid to a stop on the grass. Suzanna can ride a unicycle as easy as most kids can walk, but she needed a bicycle basket for the paper route. She took a newspaper out of her basket and asked, "You guys running?"

"Nope, jogging," Quint said.

"Hang-gliding," I told her.

"Free-falling?" Quint asked, collapsing spread eagle on the ground.

Suzanna looked annoyed. "I mean, how about running in the *Examiner*'s new contest? It tells all about it in today's paper."

Quint lay there on the ground with his eyes closed, fake laughing. "Come on, Suze, tell us the truth. How much extra do they pay you to push those stupid contests?"

"Forget it," I told her. "Thanks, but no thanks." The *Examiner* is our town's newspaper. It's *always* having contests about something. In the fall it's an Apple Pie Recipe Contest. Last winter they had a Snow Person Building Contest. Sometimes they just put photographs in the paper to see who can tell what the picture is of—stuff like very close close-ups of paper clips or an ant's eye. Once my brother won

13

their Piano Playing Contest, though, and they gave him this really neat Scott Joplin record.

My dad says the *Examiner* has all these contests because the rest of the news they print is so dull. I guess they can't report much good detective stuff— like poisonings and stabbings and jewel heists, like in the big city. I mean, Pittsfield only has 9,327 people, not counting the farmers, of course, because they're not in the city limits.

Suzanna's OK, though. I didn't want to hurt her feelings. I decided to ask her, "What's it for this time?"

"You're probably right. It's no good for either of you. It's a Superkids Contest," she said, dangling the paper in front of me. "Changed your mind?"

"No joke? They're looking for a Superkid?" Quint asked. He snatched up one of his beer cans and balanced it on top of his head. "Then they're looking for me." He sat there without moving, like a statue. "Quentin A. Superkid, in person." He bowed low, and the can bounced off onto the grass.

"Do you have to play the saxophone or swallow swords or something like that?" I asked Suzanna.

"Try reading the rules," she said. "Page three." She threw me Dad's paper, popped a wheelie to show off, and sped away.

I rolled the rubber band off the paper and onto my wrist. We sat down on the old green park bench and I turned to page three.

"Here it is," I announced. " 'Superkids Contest, sponsored by the Pittsfield *Examiner*. Contest open to Pittsfield sixth graders.' That's us, all right. 'Two winners will be chosen, one boy and one girl.' "

"Let me see that," Quint said, grabbing the paper. Then he read, in one breath, " 'Contestants must submit a one-page essay describing their hobby or special interest. The newspaper will select the finalists, and winners will be chosen by a vote of the Central School sixth graders on Tuesday, May 18, after an assembly at which the finalists will speak.' " He put the paper down and started drumming on a can. "That could be running the hundred or tossing the Frisbee, almost anything."

Just then my little sister Julia came running across the street. Julia is five. She's got stubby brown pigtails, same color as my hair. Like me, she's little for her age. On her it's cute. On me it's shrimpy.

"Harvey!" she yelled. "Mom said you should push me on the swings." She gives orders a lot.

"Later," I told her. "I'm busy."

"I'll go home and tell," she said. She would, too. She's a tiger.

I went over and lifted her into a swing and did an underdog, running under and pushing her as high as I could. She was laughing like crazy.

Then it came to me. Just like that. I turned to Julia and said, "Hey, I've got my beer cans. I'm a Superkid."

15

"OK, Superkid," she yelled. "Push me higher."

"Say, Quint," I called, trying hard to keep myself from leaping into the air and clicking my heels together. "I'm going to enter. I've got my beer-can collection. I bet anything I can win with it."

"Not bad," he said, yawning at the idea. "Not good enough, but not totally bad."

"Listen, Quint," I told him, "I've got 798 cans, not counting the ones I just traded you. I've got more beer cans than anybody in this town. And I can get a lot more. I'll get a thousand, two thousand cans."

Quint wasn't listening to me at all. He went sprinting to the sandpile and did a running broad jump into the pit, taking the tower off some kid's sand castle. The kid hauled back and hit him with his shovel, but Quint didn't seem to notice. He sauntered back with a funny smile and leaned over close to my ear. "Magic," he whispered slow, like he was casting a spell or something. "I'll use magic."

I could see this thick yellow poison stuff steaming out of big black kettles, but Quint just reached in his jeans pocket and took out a beat-up deck of cards. He riffled them like a pro.

"Pick a card," he ordered, "any card." I did. It was the Queen of Diamonds. I put it back in the deck, and then, easy and slow, he made that Queen of Diamonds rise straight up and out of the middle of those cards until I could see her whole head.

"Fabulous," he sighed. "Fabulous."

I'd seen him fooling around like that before. It

16

was just tricks, though. "Sure, Quint," I told him. "It's good."

"It's better than good," he said. "It's great. What do I win?"

"What do *I* win, you mean," I answered, and Quint gave a big horse laugh. I read on. " 'Fifteen dollars in cash—' "

"Not enough," Quint cut in. "Keep going."

" '—and a ten-dollar gift certificate from the Hobby Hutch—' "

"The what? I never heard of it."

"Me neither," I told him. " 'The Hobby Hutch, Pittsfield's new hobby store, holding its grand opening Saturday.' And, listen, Quint—this is great. 'The Pittsfield *Examiner* will donate a trophy case to Central School.' And the first trophies in it are going to be twenty-inch Superkid cups—with the winners' *names* engraved on them."

Quint's face turned grim, and he stood up straight like he was leading the Pledge of Allegiance. "Harv," he said, "I've decided to win this contest." He grabbed his bike and tossed the cans into his basket. "Race you to the newspaper office. Bet I'm the first to sign up." And away he went.

"Push me again, Superkid," Julia yelled from the swing. "I died down. Push me again."

I reached for my cans and my skateboard and ran over to give Julia another swing. Then I followed fast after Quint.

It isn't a long way—six blocks or so—to the town

square where the newspaper office is. It's pretty fast going on a skateboard, too, if you don't hit Brown's shoe factory just when they're closing for the day. I skimmed down the sidewalk on Maple, swerving around most of the big cracks like on a slalom course, past the Methodist Church and the parsonage. I was just turning the corner at the shoe factory when I almost had a head-on with another kid on a skateboard.

"Trumble!" Eric Wagner shouted. "You're a menace on wheels." Eric's this guy in my class who showed me how to skateboard.

"Hey, look, I'm sorry," I told him. "Just had a crummy teacher."

"You're not so bad for a kid with two left legs," he said, and laughed. "Where you going?"

I didn't know whether to tell him or not. What if *everybody* entered the contest? Just what if? "Oh, down to the courthouse," I said. "Thought I'd skateboard around it. Give those old guys sitting on benches something to talk about." We've got this fancy hundred-year-old courthouse in the middle of the square, and every afternoon these same old men sit outside it and smoke and talk and watch the people go by. They don't like kids a whole lot. "I just thought it might be fun."

"I'd come with you, but I got a piano lesson. Listen, if you push off right at the bottom of the courthouse steps, it's downhill enough to give you a really good start. See you around."

18

I stuck the skateboard under my arm and walked the rest of the way. When I went into the newspaper office, I saw that Quint wasn't there. But his name was on the sheet the lady had me sign. Ours were the only names.

So what if Quint beat me to the sign-up? I was sure my beer cans were better than a curly lip and magic any old day.

2 · Avalanche

In bed that night I thought about all the kids who'd see my name on a big gold trophy shining in its new glass case. And they'd see my picture in the paper, too. "Hey, that's Harvey," they'd yell. "I know Harvey Trumble. Everybody knows him. He's got more beer cans than anybody in the world. I bet if he stacked his collection up in two big piles, King Kong would think they were the World Trade Center." And I could see the old Goodyear blimp pulling this long glowing sign through the night sky. *Harvey Trumble, Harvey Trumble*, it flashed in red, white, and blue lights. It was beautiful.

But then, when the pictures went away, I wondered if I really did have enough cans. In the dark I could hear my gerbils scuttling around in their cage and spinning their ferris wheel. I could faintly make out my beer cans in stacks around the room. They were in alphabetical order—from Acme to Van Merritt.

I hadn't told Quint the truth, though. I didn't have 798 cans at all. It was closer to 600, and a lot of them doubles. I don't even know why I told Quint I had so many. Maybe the contest judges would count. Maybe somebody would find out I was lying. If I could make a lot of good trades and hustle around, I thought, everybody would realize it was a *serious* collection.

Still, even though it was midnight, I couldn't close my eyes. I needed a plan. Quint was so sure he would win. It was hard for me to be that sure. There was only one thing to do—fix myself a thick peanut-butter toast to help me think. My brain needed quick energy. I got up in the dark and tiptoed quietly across the cold floor.

Suddenly, I was flying. I was a rocket and I could see the stars to prove it. Somehow, I'd stepped down smack in the middle of my skateboard. It shot backwards, flung me forward, and slammed us both headfirst into four-foot stacks of beer cans. Those cans dominoed over and touched off more piles, which set off still more, and the avalanche just kept on going. A to V, all my cans were lying there scattered on the floor. Then, for maybe a whole minute, it was very, very quiet.

My big brother Peter snapped on the light. "You all right, Harvey?" he asked, his eyes half-open. There I was on the floor in my Green Bay Packers pajamas, with beer cans heaped around my feet, rubbing my head. As soon as he focused in on me, Peter closed his eyes, shook his head, and said, very quiet and steady, "Harvey, why don't you grow up?" He staggered out, slamming the door so hard the cans clanged all over again, arranging themselves in new heaps.

Julia opened the door next, sniffling and stumbling in, dragging her stuffed owl Zachary by his wing. She did what she always does when she's mad and sleepy at the same time. She yowled like a siren. Then she started pounding me on the head with that crazy owl.

I was pulling myself up off the floor to swat her one, when my mom and dad appeared together, blinking at the light. At first they just stood there in their

nightclothes, staring. They took in the floor and then me, being beaten up with an owl by this runny-nosed kid.

"Oh, Harvey." Mom sighed, as though this was going to hurt her a lot more than it did me. She picked up Julia and Zachary and stumbled through the cans toward the door. "Harvey, Harvey," she went on, sounding like a record I'd heard before. "I think you should collect stamps. You can keep them in books, on shelves." As she left, I could hear her still talking through Julia's shrieks. "It's an excellent hobby, very quiet." She didn't shout, I guess, because she knew my father would.

He did, too. He blew his stack.

"Harvey Trumble," he roared, "you listen to me!" He kept pointing his finger at me to make sure I knew who he was talking to. "I've had just about enough of this nonsense. Those beer cans are leaving this house."

It's weird how things can strike you funny. I mean, beer cans leaving—it sounded crazy. I got this Technicolor picture in my head of all my cans sprouting legs, picking themselves up, snapping to attention, and leaving this house through the front door like some metal army. I was smart enough not to smile about it, though. The cans were just turning the corner and kicking their heels in the air when it occurred to me that he might be serious, and I realized that I'd turned the volume down. But when I switched back he was still talking loud enough to keep Julia awake. ". . . tell you right now about these cans." I hadn't missed much.

"One, they clutter up your room so it can't be properly cleaned." My father is very organized. He is always one-two-threeing things. "Two, they smell dreadful. Twelve-year-olds' bedrooms have no business smelling like a brewery." That wasn't really fair because I always washed my cans out. I really did. "Three, stacks of cans are painfully noisy when they hit the deck at midnight." From her room we could hear my sister give one last cry before plugging her mouth with her thumb. "Fourth, they make it look like I drink barrels of beer, which I don't. Fifth, and finally, I don't like them."

He reached down, picked up an Old Chicago can that had stopped at his bare toes, crunched it in half with one hand and tossed it back into the mess. My stomach churned. I figured I'd better argue, even though that hardly ever works with my dad.

"But Dad," I said. "Sir," I said, "I've been saving these cans for almost three years and I like them more than anything I've got. I do. I bet they're worth a thousand dollars easy. I ought to get twenty dollars alone for my Old Dutch cone top." I looked for it in the general direction of the O's, with no luck. I was glad that Old Chicago he'd crumpled was practically worthless. "It's here somewhere."

"Fine," replied my father, not really listening to

my grand totals. "Sell them. Or you can take them to the recycling center so they'll be put to good use again. But," he said pointing his finger in a grand sweep around my room, "I want them out of this house by Sunday night. Do you understand me?"

Reason hadn't worked. By this time I was begging. "Can't I keep the twenty-dollar ones at least, the really great ones like the Old Dutch conie and that Kato conie I got so cheap at the flea market?"

I looked around for it, but it had gone into hiding.

"Look, Harvey," he said, quieter. He was calming down. But he wasn't giving an inch. "It may say in those beer-can books of yours that you've got beer cans worth twenty dollars, but you can't tell me somebody'd pay you that. Do you know anybody who will?"

I didn't. He had me there. I didn't even know anybody who had twenty dollars to spend. So I didn't have a snappy Superman answer. I just wanted to keep my collection, all of it.

Dad closed the door quietly, leaving his midnight fury right there in the room with me and my banned cans. I decided to forget about the peanut-butter toast and get some sleep. So I waded through the clanking cans and climbed into my bed, an island in the middle of a rolling metal sea.

3 · The Gold Gazebo

We've got this gazebo in our backyard. It's a one-room summer house with lots of screens and fancy woodwork. On top its pointed green roof is a one-legged iron rooster that turns with the wind.

Early that Saturday morning after Dad banished my beer cans, I was sitting in the gazebo leafing through my beer-can book and eating a stack of peanut-butter toast. I was thinking about my poor cans and about the contest I couldn't win. No light bulbs were flashing over my head. My brain was stuck in neutral.

All of a sudden a terrific crash shook the roof of the gazebo and sent my plate of toast careening across the floor. Shingles from the roof zoomed down past the screen window. My teeth clanged together.

"It's a tornado!" I heard a kid scream.

"Tornado? Geez, it's a hurricane!" somebody else yelled, and the roof of the gazebo shook again. I leaped into the disaster drill squat they make us do at school—curled up with my arms over my head—clamped my eyes shut, and waited for a twister to lift me straight up by the hair.

"Spin, chicken, spin!" the first kid screamed, and the roof trembled again.

Chicken? Even if the tornado had hit a farm outside town, would a chicken still be spinning when it reached here? Anyway, who'd yell at it to keep going?

Suddenly I remembered it was a nice day. The sun was shining. But it didn't hurt to be cautious. So, carefully, I unwound myself and opened my eyes just far enough to see that the leaves on the big maple tree weren't even moving.

"Billy, help me! I'm falling!" The cry was coming from the gazebo roof.

"Grab hold of the edge, klutz," somebody else above me yelled. First I saw a pair of dirty sneakers dangle off the roof, and then the kid in them dropped into my mom's purple lilac bush. Something cracked. I hoped it was his leg and not the bush.

"What'd you have to do that for?" the kid on top yelled as he jumped off the roof. He landed right next to the first guy, who was rolling in the grass, moaning. It was Billy and Simon, the Terrible Two. They're eight, going on nine, and both of them live in the next block. They're always put in different classes because no teacher at Central School could handle both of them.

"Cut it out. I know you're faking," Billy said.

"I am not," groaned Simon. "I skinned my elbow and besides, I may also have a brain concussion."

"Not unless your brains are in your toes," said Billy. "You landed on your feet."

27

"Just what do you little vandals think you're do-ing?" I demanded. "My father will sue you." Dad was always *saying* he was going to sue somebody—people who didn't pay their bills at his drugstore or guys who delivered him junky hairbrushes with bristles that fell out. "If you hurt the roof, my dad—"

Simon tried to blow on his bleeding elbow. "*It's* not hurt. I am." Simon has a tangle of curly brown hair and thick glasses that make his eyes look big. And he really uses them. He gave me that look of total innocence he always gives grown-ups when he's in trouble. "We were just climbing your maple tree when we saw that weather vane. We never noticed it before."

"So we jumped on the roof and started spinning that chicken around," Billy said. Billy is a funny-looking kid. Four of his bottom teeth are out and his sandy blond hair is very, very short. His mother really sheared him the last time he got bubble gum stuck in it. Billy has more nerve than Simon, and he looked right at me and *smiled.* "You should have seen that bird go," he said, twirling himself around like a top. "Come on up, I'll show you." He started to climb back up.

"Get down here!" I boomed. "You guys leave, will you, while this place is still in one piece!" I yelled at them through the screen.

"This sure is a creepy place," Billy said, pushing open the screen door and walking right in. "Too dark for me."

"Good-bye," I said, trying to push him back out.

Simon stuck his head in the door and looked around. "What's all that lumber for?" he asked, slamming the door behind him.

"None of your business," I said. "Get lost, you guys."

"But we need some wood," Billy said.

"Well, you can't have this. Dad got it off a friend of his last summer, and he started to make this place into a playhouse for my sister."

"Not a bad idea," Simon said, pacing around. "But it's dark as the inside of a cat's stomach."

I flicked on the light in the peak of the ceiling. "Dad wired that up there," I told them.

"Why didn't he finish it?" Billy asked, pounding his fists on the boarded-up windows to see if they could take it. "It looks weird this way, half open and half shut."

"He just quit one day," I explained. "Julia kept complaining about the mosquitoes and spiders, and how spooky it gets, and how maybe there are ghosts out here and sharks."

"It sure is a waste," Billy said, picking up a loose board. "We could use this wood to build a tree house. We're good at building things."

"Forget it, guys," I said, opening the door to let them out. "It's time to move on to the next roof."

"Harvey, why do you want to get rid of us?" Billy said, tossing his ball in the air and not moving an inch toward the open door.

"Yeah," Simon said. "We're really great once you get to know us."

Great? Those two kids had reputations. They were pesty. Breaking windows or arms. Running over somebody's prize roses or riding through wet concrete. You were never sure what they'd do, so you had to be very careful. I kept the door open and waited.

"I'm not going to waste all day with you two, not with my big beer-can problem staring me in the face. If you're not out in five seconds I'm going to use some of that lumber on you."

"Beer cans?" breathed Billy. "You drink *beer?* That's against the law."

"We won't tell a soul," Simon said seriously. Billy crossed his heart and nodded.

"Knock it off, you guys," I told them. "For your information, I don't drink the beer. I collect the empty cans."

I could tell they didn't believe me. "You got to be kidding," Billy said. "What do you do that for?"

Since they asked, I closed the door and decided to tell them all about my collection. I'll tell *anybody* about it. I said I had a *thousand* cans. I'm not sure why I kept making the number bigger. I guess I figured that they were just little kids and didn't know much about numbers, so I rounded off to the nearest thousand. I told them about the midnight avalanche and the shouting match with my dad. I even told them about the contest.

"What's he want you to do with a thousand beer cans?" Simon asked. "Did he have any suggestions?"

"Sure, he had lots of suggestions." I'd been going over them in my head when Billy and Simon tornadoed me. "He said I could sell them for junk. But I don't *want* to sell them. I like them. Besides, they'll probably be worth enough to put me through college if I keep them long enough. I figure if I sell them to collectors I could get one or two thousand dollars for them, easy."

"A thousand dollars?"

"You're kidding. For *cans*?"

"No joke. I can prove it," I said. I picked up my trusty beer-can book and showed it to them. "Ever seen one of these?"

"No. We don't collect things," Billy said. "We're too busy."

"Look, I'll show you." I leafed through the pages of beer-can pictures. "See this Blackhawk can here? I've got that. See right after its name, it's got a 6/1? That means it's worth six ordinary cans—cans like this Hamm's—see?"

"Sure we see," Simon nodded. "How much is the ordinary guy—Hamm's—worth?"

I leafed through the book to show them how official it looked. "I don't want you guys to think I'm kidding you, so I'm going to show you where it's written right here in the book. Look. It says, 'The base can has a value of fifty cents.' Naturally, that's when it's in good shape. The Hamm's is a base can."

31

"You're trying to tell us that a regular old beer can is worth fifty cents?" Simon said. "Sure, sure." He didn't believe a word of it.

"No lie. I swear."

"You mean your Blackhawk can," Simon figured, "is worth six times fifty cents. *Three dollars?* Three dollars for one smelly old beer can? And you've got a thousand of them? Wow, you've got a mint in there."

"I know, I know. Now why don't you guys go away, so I can decide how to keep from losing my fortune." I flung open the door again, and since they didn't go outside, I did. I slammed the door and sat down on the step.

"Harv, I've got it," Simon called out. "This is what you do. First off, you get yourself lots of those huge black plastic bags. Put your cans inside. Then you move them all right out here into your gazebo."

It was such a dumb idea I couldn't believe it, but I went back inside and looked around anyway. "That wouldn't work," I told him. "They'd get soaked when it rains. They rust, you know."

"No, they wouldn't," Billy jumped in. He grabbed the board he'd been sitting on and ran over to a screened window to see if it fit. "All we have to do is close in the rest of these sides. We've already got a light up there that's bright enough for cans."

I had to admit the idea had possibilities. Tomorrow was the deadline for getting the cans out of the house, and the gazebo *was* out of the house. One problem, though. The rest of the sides had to be boarded up. I wasn't going to move my cans out into the rain, no sir. There was only one answer—child labor.

"You guys think you're pretty smart, don't you?" I paused to let the compliment sink in. "Well," I continued, "there's no way it could be fixed up by tomorrow."

"Come on, let us try." Simon was practically jumping up and down with excitement. All those kids wanted to do was build something and I had something that needed building. I was a little worried about them wrecking the place and themselves, but I had no choice. I decided I had to go all the way.

"Well, OK," I said, trying to look cool, "but no funny stuff."

"We can do it, Harv," Billy said, giving me that smile with the missing teeth. I shuddered. "We've even got some gold paint in our basement," he said. "It's left over from the Jaycees' Fourth of July float last year. My dad was chairman."

"Gold? A solid gold gazebo? That's really different," I said, trying to smile back. Actually, it didn't sound half bad.

"That'll make you the beer-can champion, all right," Billy said.

"Champion? I'll be king," I declared.

Simon giggled and scratched his head. "Well, Your Majesty," he said, climbing up the stack of boards. "You be king and we'll be knights."

"We'll need swords," Billy said. "And a catapult

for invaders. Maybe some pots of boiling oil."

Simon had reached the top of the lumber pile and was waving his arms, making proclamations. "Attention, serfs and peasants," he yelled. "I am Sir Simon, a knight most fearful and brave. All cheer." We did. Satisfied, he stopped proclaiming and sat down to blow on his elbow some more. "Sir Billy sounds silly," he went on. "You'll have to be Sir Bill or Sir William. Too bad there aren't any dragons for us to slay. You got any enemies, Harv?"

Somehow, the whole thing was sounding very good indeed. In fact, I could see my name shining across the sky again, like a meteor. "Listen to this, you knights," I told them grandly. "I'm going to win that contest, and I'm going to wear a gold crown when the newspaper takes my picture."

"Can we start building now?" Simon asked.

"Sure," I told him. "Well, maybe. I think I'll call Dad at the drugstore. He'll like it. I know he will. He's always trying to get me to do carpenter stuff. Then we can go get some hammers and nails. Simon, you come with me. Billy, you get the boards sorted out and we'll start to pound, all three of us. We'll turn this place into a real palace, a solid gold castle for me, Harvey Trumble, the Beer Can King."

"All hail," Simon said.

4 · The End of the Rainbow

"Yipe!" Simon scored a direct thumb hit for about the tenth time. His fingernails were like magnets. We'd worked all morning and past lunch hitting nails, missing nails, bending them in half. Every time I said, "We'll never make it," Simon yelled, "We will," and Billy pounded faster. Finally, with the end in sight, Billy cut out to get the paint. Before too long Simon moaned, "I'm quitting," and tossed the hammer on the floor. "Billy's been gone half an hour. If he stopped to eat, I'll blast him." He slammed the door and sat down on the gazebo step.

Looking out across the yard I could see Billy pulling the wagon full of paint through the garden, squashing a row of yellow tulips.

"Good grief!" I yelled, running out to meet him. "Don't murder the flowers. Mom talks to those tulips. She read somewhere that flowers grow better if you talk nice to them. It won't work if their heads are off."

Billy turned and looked down at the flowers. "Hey, you guys, shape up." He squatted down to see what would happen. Then he turned to me. "What does she say to them?"

"She tells them they're looking good. She tells them they're going to grow up to be big and strong."

"Flowers won't listen to junk like that," Billy said, getting up and pulling the wagon across the grass. "It doesn't work with me, and I've got ears."

"Just in case," I told him, "use the sidewalk next time."

"How's it going?" Billy asked.

"We're all done," I told him. "I just pounded in the last board and Simon just finished off his thumb. There's still a crack or two between the slats, but we can always patch those up. Come on in and look around."

Billy stuck his head in and shuddered. "Geez, it's more like a dungeon now than a castle," he said. "Maybe we should put in a few torture instruments. How about a dentist's chair in the middle of the room?"

"What took you?" Simon asked. He sat on the step and watched his fingernail turn color.

"How'd you make out, Billy?" I asked. "You want to start painting now or later?"

"Maybe never," Billy said. "The paint's all wrong."

Simon was sucking his purple thumb. "Wass wong wiff it?" he asked.

There were lots of paint cans there in the wagon. I could see them. "Isn't there enough?"

"Sure, there's *enough*," he told us, pulling the wagon up in front of us. "I've got seven cans and three brushes. But it'll look crummy if we use it.

There was only one can of gold on the shelf. The rest are left over from different projects. Each one is a different color. Our castle won't be solid gold at all, or solid red or solid blue or solid green or even plain white. It'll look like an explosion in a paint factory."

"I hate it," I told him.

"No, listen, you guys, that's cool," Simon said, leaping up and forgetting his bum thumb. "Here's what we do. First off, we paint one wall gold and put Harvey's throne there."

"My what, where?" I hadn't said anything about a throne.

"A king's gotta have a throne," Simon explained. "At the A & P we can get some grapefruit crates. We'll make it out of those. They're not too strong, but they're wood, at least. We can paint the throne gold, too," Simon decided. I could see what they were doing. They were trying to take over my gazebo.

"I've *got* it!" Billy cut in. "Then we make these huge rainbows on the *other* walls. We'll use up all the rest of the paint on great big rainbows. I brought some paint along called Sunset Orange and Peppermint Pink."

"Neat," Simon said. "Perfect. And the beer cans . . . We'll stack the beer cans at the end of the rainbows. Get it? Get it, Harvey? They're the treasure. You get it, Harvey?"

"Sure, I *get* it," I told him. "Except I don't like

you little kids telling me what I'm going to do. Maybe I've got some other ideas for my castle and my throne. Maybe I don't want any Peppermint Pink rainbows."

"Why not?" Simon demanded. "Don't you think it'll be cool to have a heap of cans at the end of the rainbow? You said they were worth a lot, didn't you?"

"Look," Billy said in his mean-kid voice, "it's all the paint we've got in the basement. If you don't want it, I'll take it home." And he would have too, right back across the tulips. It sounded like a threat to me. Besides, I kind of liked the throne and the rainbow stuff.

"Don't panic," I told him. "It's OK. Look, it's gotta be one o'clock. You guys go eat lunch so Simon won't turn to bones and I'll meet you back here around three. My castle will be ready for its treasure tomorrow."

I made a big sweeping bow to them. They broke up, bowed back, and then galloped across the backyard, vaulting the tulips and the rosebushes. I heard Simon telling Billy how they were going to hang a sun from the ceiling. Over my dead body. Bossy kids.

Suddenly Julia came barreling out of the house. "Guess who got a letter?" she yelled.

"You," I guessed. "You finally got an answer from Santa Claus. Did he tell you why he didn't bring you that doll you saw on television?"

"He's too busy," she snapped. "Guess again."

"It's from the President. He wants Peter to be the first astronaut to play the piano in space."

"You're just teasing," she said, flapping the envelope back and forth. Then she stopped, stared at the boarded-up gazebo, and glared back at me. "How come you've been in my playhouse?" she demanded. "Who said you could do stuff to it?"

"Dad said," I told her. "I called him at the store. He said I could use your old playhouse because you don't."

"I do, too. You can't have it. It's mine."

"Look, Julia, we're going to fix it up like a castle and maybe you can be a princess or something." She didn't scream, so I figured the princess part did it. "Who got the letter? Was it me?"

She started dancing around again, waving it in the air. "Harvey got a letter," she sang. "Harvey got a letter. Scaredy Cat, Scaredy Cat, don't know where the letter's at." She hid it behind her.

I picked her up and took it away. She was getting ready to put on the old fountain-of-tears act, so I said, "Say, go look at our gazebo. This afternoon we're going to paint it with rainbows."

"Mother says you'd better eat now," she announced, wandering into my dark castle. I didn't need to worry about her. She was scared of the dark and I could hear the mosquitoes hum.

I tore the letter open. It was from the editor of the *Examiner*:

Dear Harvey,
We have received your application for the

Pittsfield *Examiner*'s Superkids Contest. We are pleased that you are entering and would like you to send us, by Friday, May 7, an essay describing the hobby or special interest in which you excel.

When your essay is received, we will make an appointment with you to have a reporter come to your home to interview you and take pictures for the paper.

Finalists in the contest will be announced in the newspaper on Monday, May 17.

Good luck.

Sincerely,
George Adams

This contest was like an obstacle course. First, I gave them my application. Now the second jump was an essay. I guessed a lot of kids would drop out right away as soon as they had to write something, but not me. As I ate my chicken noodle soup, I read the letter again and tried to think of a few good things to say. I put three choice beer cans in front of me for inspiration, got out some notebook paper, and started to write:

COLLECTING BEER CANS

by Harvey Trumble

My hobby is collecting ~~empty~~ beer cans. I have ~~almost a thousand about eight hundred~~ hundreds of them in a ~~castle~~ gazebo in my back yard. I fixed up the gazebo like a castle and painted it gold inside with rainbows all around. I decided to put rainbows there because then the beer cans look like the treasure at the end of the rainbows. They are a ~~very big~~ really fantastic collection. They are worth a lot more than ~~two thousand~~ a thousand dollars. I learn about what they ~~——~~ are worth from reading beer can books.

This hobby is a ~~good~~ fabulous one because it is fun to collect cans and trade with other kids. Also it is good for the ecology because I clean up pollution when I pick up cans from the ground and out of the lake. This is a fantastic hobby and I excel in it.

I would like a reporter to see my beer can collection, my castle, and my gold throne.

Me, reporters, and a gold throne. Not bad. I stuck the essay in my pocket for copying over and ran as fast as I could out to the castle. Julia was sitting on the step, waiting.

"Can I see the rainbows?" she asked.

"Can you ever." I clicked the light on. "Just watch." I opened the paint cans with a screwdriver and set to work. I couldn't remember the way colors go in a rainbow, but I figured it didn't matter much since rainbows don't have Avocado Green and Peppermint Pink in them anyway. I made a small green half-circle, cleaned the brush off a little, dipped it in the Sunset Orange, and spread that on right above the green. Then I stepped back to take a look.

"It's beautiful," Julia said. "It's just beautiful. Harvey, do all rainbows drip?"

The orange paint was drooling down in little streams onto the green stripe. It looked rippled, like mountain brooks. It looked cool. But I decided to use less paint for the blue so the whole rainbow wouldn't ooze. Next, I sloshed on an enormous arc of red, and, above that, one of Peppermint Pink. By the time I got to the white stripe, I had to stand on the ladder. The smell of paint was so strong it almost made me sick. But the whole gazebo was changed. It was magnificent. You never saw a rainbow like it.

"Do another one," Julia begged. And I did. I kept on splashing up arches of wild, glorious color, and Julia kept on clapping.

5 · "Officer, Arrest Those Boys"

"Do you need another bag, Harvey?" Mom called up the stairs.

"Nope. The cans are all in sacks now. We'll take them out as soon as Quint shows up," I yelled back. "Only trouble here is the mice. Poor guys don't know where to go now I've pulled down their house. Shoo, mouse!" I shouted. My mom has this thing about mice. It all started when a couple of them got in the basement once and ate holes in this gingerbread house she was saving for Christmas.

"Harvey William Trumble, if you've brought another mouse into your room . . ."

"Just a joke, Mom," I told her. "Can't you take a joke?" Actually, I had once carried a mouse home from the dump in an old Falstaff can. He'd built a little grass nest in it, but I didn't know he was there till I got home. He and Mom were both glad when I took him back to his family.

The doorbell rang and it was Quint. I'd asked him to come over and help carry the cans out to my castle. I didn't need the help really, but I wanted to see his face when he took a look at the rainbows.

"Hey, I heard Eric Wagner's running," he told me right away.

"No kidding. What's he doing?" I asked him.

"Skateboarding. Remember his handstand push-ups going down Suicide Hill?" We took the steps two at a time up to my room. "You hear anything?" he asked me.

"Nope. I've been too busy getting my place ready. Haven't talked to anybody. What else do you know?"

"Well, Michael Holt might enter with his drums, and somebody said Matthew Marrinson was thinking about trying out with bird calls. I don't know about any others. You mail in your essay yet?"

"Yes. This morning," I told him. "How about you?"

"I mailed it on the way over. I got things all planned out. I'm going to have a fantastic block circus this Saturday in my backyard," he said, grabbing three cans from a big pile of doubles I had lying on my bed—some Schlitz, Lite, Budweisers—the kind I could collect a dozen of every day. He started juggling them high. "I'm going to be ringmaster, magician, and juggler. I'm a real pro." He missed one, so he let the others go crashing down with it to the floor. It didn't matter. I'd probably just toss them in the garbage anyway. "There'll be some other acts, too—dancing, clowns, a cat parade, stuff like that. Anyway, I told the paper that would be the best time for pictures."

"If it doesn't rain," I said, wondering if pictures of my beer cans would really look as good as pictures of his circus.

"It wouldn't dare," he said.

We carried the can-filled bags down the steps like two Santa Clauses on Christmas Eve.

"I'll give you boys some nice, warm brownies and a glass of milk when you're finished," Mom said, using her best bribe.

"Ho, ho, ho," Quint chortled as he shifted the weight to his other shoulder. Mom held up the brownies, still hot in the pan, and I could almost taste the chocolate.

The promise of food set us running across the backyard with our packs. I opened the door of the castle for Quint, snapped on the light, and stepped back so he could take a look. He gasped.

The rainbows were like huge hills of color waving around the room. It almost made you dizzy. At the end of one of them I'd already stacked a small pyramid of cans. They glittered in the light like the cars parked in used car lots. Swinging down from the light bulb was the big foil sun that Billy and Simon had made, and their grapefruit crate throne sat square in the middle of the gold wall across from the door. I walked over, sat down on the throne, and said, "You like it?"

I thought Quint was going to flip. "It looks like Oz," he said. "It really does."

"Dad put a lock on the door for me last night," I told him. "I was afraid somebody would just walk right in and rip off my cans. What do you think, though?"

"Never saw anything like it," he said, shaking his head. "What made you dream up all this stuff anyway? The rainbows and that crazy gold chair?"

"Well," I told him, "it's mostly because I've decided to be a Beer Can King. How's that for a title?" Quint was impressed. I could tell it. And that meant he was running scared. Boy, did I feel great. Grandly, I leaned back in my throne. The pine slats squeaked ominously. Figuring that falling on my bottom would put a quick end to my majesty, I jumped up fast.

Quint laughed and got that cocky winner's look again.

"Hey, I'm gonna stack the cans at the ends of all the rainbows," I told him, heading over to the one I'd finished.

"Like pots of gold?" He was still grinning, but I couldn't tell whether it was because he liked it or because he thought it was funny.

"G-e-r-o-n-i-m-o," yelled a voice that could only be Billy's. The roof shivered like I'd felt it shiver before and the light bulb in the ceiling flickered and went out. Standing there in the dark, Quint and I could hear him sing, "Round and round she goes and where she stops nobody knows . . ."

At least I didn't panic again and curl up on the floor. But before I could catch my breath to shout at Billy, Simon called him from way across the yard.

"Come on," he yelled. "Get back over here and help me drag this wagon. That weather vane is gonna fly off there if you're not careful."

The thud of Billy's jump to the ground shook us again in the darkness. We made our way to the door and looked out.

"What's going on?" Quint demanded.

Billy was roaring across the grass, yelling, "Stop! Stop it! Don't kill them. Listen, no more murder!"

Simon stopped, expecting, I guess, a land mine at least. He was right at the border of our garden.

Billy held his hand up like a traffic cop. "You gotta go around the flowers. You gotta use the sidewalk. Those flowers *talk* to Harvey's mom. Harvey was mad as a hornet at me for cutting some of their heads off the other day."

The wagon was piled high with junk. It really did need two people to keep it together. Billy broadjumped over the flowers and they started off to the sidewalk.

"What's with Billy and Simon?" Quint asked again.

"They've been helping," I said as they raced toward us with their rolling heap. "They're not so bad. I've made them my knights."

As they pulled up in front of Quint and me, Simon said, "Wait'll you see it. Just wait'll you see. It was like magic finding this thing just when we needed it." He reached in the wagon and lifted out a fabulous breastplate of armor. It was real, solid, genuine, nonphony armor, not the stuff you make out of foil for Halloween. It was museum real.

"Come on, where'd you guys get that armor?" I demanded.

48

"In an alley."

"An alley?" Quint and I said together.

"It was just lying there with some rags and newspapers. Great, right?" Simon asked.

"Great, wrong," I told him. "Nobody's about to throw that thing away."

"Well, they did," Billy said. "It was there all by itself. Nobody was guarding it." He shined it with his shirtsleeve and put it back in the wagon.

"And, you guys, look at this," Simon said. "This is even better. Billy and me are gonna start can collecting, too. An old guy was throwing them out as garbage."

"In an alley, too?" I asked.

"Sure, an alley. What's wrong with alleys? The old man said he was cleaning his basement. He said he was moving to Florida and getting rid of junk like old clothes and bottles and beer cans," Simon explained. "We're going back to get some magazines and a washtub full of pop bottles. He told us we could have them."

Simon took the sack out and dumped at least twenty cans on the grass—*half of them cone-tops!* They could have been diamonds, they were so beautiful. I'd never seen them before in real life. They were like movie stars. You don't know for sure if they're real since you've only seen them in pictures. As far as I could tell, the conies were all from Minnesota. Four or five of them were Grain Belt. There was a Royal Bohemian, a Regal, and the rest were Rex. I knew the

49

books listed them all at around 20-to-1. Pure gold. They'd gotten some rusty old punch-tops, too, worth something, but nothing like those cone-tops.

"You guys hit it rich!" I shouted.

"Are they good ones?" Simon asked.

"They're great," I went on. "Why, *any* conies you find . . ."

"Look," Quint cut in, pushing me off to the side. "I bet Harv here will trade you some brand-new Schlitz and Pabst Blue Ribbon cans for those old cone-tops." I couldn't believe it. Quint was trying to get those cans for me. He must have known I'd give anything to get them. "Those punch-tops are rusty and old," he went on, "and really worth a lot. I bet he'd even give you some naval jelly to clean the rust off."

"*Navel* jelly?" Simon snickered. Billy bent over in dirty-joke-type giggles.

"Will you babies grow up," Quint told them. "Anyway, it's not belly-button navel. It's navy naval. They use this stuff in the navy to get rust off boats. But it works good for those valuable beer cans, too. Right, Harv?"

"Sure," I said, beginning to get a funny feeling inside that this wasn't a red-hot idea. I couldn't get over Quint helping me out. Why would he want to do that?

"Will you give us some of it?" Simon asked.

"You've got some to trade, don't you?" Quint asked, winking.

"Sure I do, but . . ."

"Sir Knights," Quint declared. "Your king will give you, absolutely free of charge, a bottle of naval jelly and a bag of—how many, Harv, twenty-five cans?" I nodded. "Twenty-five brand new assorted cans—Schlitz, Lite, Buds, Old Milwaukees—and you won't have to clean them up at all. You just give Harvey those ten cone-tops. That's better than two-to-one. Right, Harv?"

"Right," I echoed him. "Better than two-to-one. It's a great trade." I didn't say great for who.

"It's a deal, then," Quint said.

"Look," Simon asked me, "these cans you're trading us, what are they worth, anyway?"

"What do you want me to do, get my book?" I asked, hoping he wouldn't say yes.

Simon shrugged his shoulders. "I guess not."

"Of course not," Quint said. "Harvey's OK. You just built a castle with him. You can trust him. Shake on it."

The way Quint talked it sounded like he was practicing to be a circus barker for Saturday. It was pure cotton candy and they were eating it up. Billy stuck out his hand and we shook. "Are the cans in the castle?" he asked.

"I left all the doubles upstairs," I said, not sure whether I should feel like a millionaire or a rat.

"Then Harv and me'll go get them," Quint announced. "You kids just sort out the punch-tops for yourselves. They're the ones that somebody's opened with a can opener. They don't make them like that anymore. They're antiques."

"Are they worth four-to-one?" Simon asked.

"At least," Quint told them. "Come on, you guys, Harvey and me'll be back in a couple of minutes."

As we walked to the house, I decided I couldn't do it. "I just can't cheat Billy and Simon like that," I told Quint.

"What do you mean?" he said. "They're just little kids. They'd rather have new cans. Listen, you need the cans and they don't. It's that simple. Don't worry about it because they'll never find out anyway. No way they're gonna find out. Besides, if you're gonna impress anybody with your collection, you're gonna need more cans than we carried outside today. You do what I tell you and maybe you'll make it to the finals."

I didn't say anything. He was still talking like the barkers at the circus, but he was right about the cans. I didn't have near enough to fill that big gazebo.

"Say," he said, suddenly, all excited, "did you notice how many of those cans had names about a king? Royal Bohemian and Regal and did you see the Rex —that means king in some language or other. It's like ESP or something." He grabbed my arm. "Can't you see," he said. "It's like those cans were meant for *you*, Harvey, the Beer Can King."

We each took a brownie on the way up. "No, listen," I told him, "I'd have to give them two or three

52

hundred of those Pabst and Schlitz cans to make it an even trade and you know it. This'd make me more like Harvey, the Rip-Off Artist."

Upstairs, I gathered all the cheap doubles into a grocery bag and stuck in a bottle of naval jelly. We walked down the stairs from my room, not at all like Santa Clauses.

"I can't do it," I told him.

"Then forget it," he said. "If you don't want to give me a run for my money, just forget it. But don't say I didn't try to help you. Just remember, those babies don't need 25-to-1 cans and you do. I'm going home and work on my circus. So long, sucker." He gave me the old skunk-smell lip curl and slammed the door behind him.

Maybe he was right. What's the harm, anyway, I thought. What Billy and Simon don't know won't hurt them. And those cans sure would help me.

I grabbed the whole plate of brownies to take outside. Billy and Simon were still in the yard, sorting. "Have a brownie," I told them. "Have two."

"We've decided we like collecting beer cans," Billy said. "Now that we've tried the alleys, we're going to go to the dump next."

"Here are your new ones," I said, "and the naval jelly." I spilled all the cans onto the grass and started stuffing the bag with my cone-tops. But those little guys looked so happy with those stupid, worthless cans that I decided, no matter what Quint said, I just couldn't go through with it. "Listen," I started. "This is just a big mistake—"

"There they are, officer. Those are the thieves!" a high shrill voice from the street cried out. A strange-looking old man with a deer-stalker's cap pulled down over his white hair came rushing toward us, a policeman following close behind. The old man stopped, grabbed the officer's arm, and glared at us from under his bushy white eyebrows. The policeman stared us down without a smile.

I thought I was going to die. The old man turned to the policeman and tugged on his arm. "I don't care how young they are. They broke the law and they should pay for it. Brats!" he shouted, letting the policeman go and moving in toward us. "Little boys didn't steal in my day. Arrest those pilfering boys, officer." And he shook his fist at us.

Mom came bursting out the back door. "Arrest *what* boys?" she demanded.

Nobody moved.

6 · Naval Jelly, Absolutely Free

"Can I help you, sir? What are you doing in our back-yard?" Mom asked.

"My dear madam, I have reason to believe that there is stolen property in your backyard," the old man said, tugging at the brim of his Sherlock Holmes hat. He was wearing an old green sweater and around his waist a flowered apron, like he'd been interrupted doing the dishes. We all knew who he was. He'd retired here from Springfield to live with his sister over on Eubank Avenue, that street where the doctor, the funeral parlor owner, and Judge Melsheimer live. The old man always looked kind of fierce.

"Those two boys are the culprits," he said. He pointed at Billy and Simon slowly, one after the other.

"Are you absolutely sure, Mr. Watson?" the police-man asked him, looking at the two little kids and then at me. "Not the other one?"

"Of course, I'm sure," he growled. "I watched the whole crime from my kitchen window. Immediately, I grabbed my hat, called the police, scoured the neigh-borhood, and now we've tracked them down." He smiled triumphantly.

55

Billy jumped to his feet and ran over to the old man. "We thought you were throwing it away," he yelled. "It was right out there in the alley with the trash. It looked good, but it looked like garbage."

I knew it. I just knew it. Those cans were too good to be true. They'd lied to me about how they got them. They'd stolen them somehow from this old man's collection. I looked over at the bag of cans. As soon as he saw them, he would tell Billy and Simon how much they were worth. And then he would make me give them back.

"Officer," I pleaded. "They're just little kids. They didn't mean anything. The cans are all here." I turned to the old man, who was shifting back and forth, fuming. "They didn't know the cans were worth anything. They honestly thought you didn't want them."

Suddenly I felt glad to get rid of those cans. That would solve the problem completely. I wouldn't have to lie to Billy and Simon anymore. "Here, they're all yours." I reached down and handed him the bag of conies.

"What do I want with that rubbish? I never saw it before," he sputtered, throwing the sack of cans at me and wiping his hands off on the apron. "Do you think I'd call the police if those ragpickers stole a bag of beer cans? It's my *armor* I want. It's seventeenth century English and it is extremely valuable."

I couldn't believe it. He didn't want the cans. I just

sat right down on the grass and held onto the bag, hoping the old man was crazy as he looked and that he was going to change his mind.

"It's part of a collection, madam," he went on. "My father gave it to me as his father had given it to him." He directed this information at my mother, as though he thought she'd be the only one to understand.

"If it's worth so much," Simon said, "why did you leave it in back of your garage on a stack of rags and newspapers?"

"If you must know,"the old man growled, "I was all set up to clean it with naval jelly when I found there was none in the garage. So I went to the kitchen to look for more."

"Did you find it?" Billy asked.

"No, and I suppose I'll have to . . . Good grief, officer, I don't have to answer to this moppet. He has to answer to *me*."

The policeman looked at Simon and Billy and then back at the old man. "Mr. Watson," he said, clamping his hand kindly on the old man's shoulder, "if your armor was sitting on a pile of newspapers and rags in the alley, I think you can understand how the boys might have reasonably thought it was refuse."

"But they ran, officer. You should have seen them run."

"We always run," Billy told him.

"Besides, we were glad we'd found the armor for our castle," Simon added.

"We wanted to hurry and show Harvey," Billy told him. "He's the king, we're the knights, and over there is our castle." Billy pointed toward the gazebo.

"These children make no sense at all, officer," Mr. Watson said.

"They mean," Mom explained, "that they're sorry. But they want you to know that it's all just a mistake."

"Here's your armor," Simon said, lifting it very carefully out of the wagon. "It's got some dents and scratches on it, but we didn't do it, honest. No lie."

The old man took the armor from him, held it up for inspection, and then he put it on, holding it firmly against his sweater, the apron underneath it flaring out like a skirt. "Of course it's got dents and scratches, young man. It's seen *battle*. It's been struck with swords. That's where it's getting rusty, right here in the dents." He poked at the places to show us.

"You want some naval jelly?" Billy asked. "You can have this, absolutely free." He handed Mr. Watson the bottle I'd given him and Simon.

"It's great armor," Simon said to him. "But I sure don't see how knights wore whole suits of that heavy stuff. Can I try it on?"

"Not now, Simon," Mom said, standing between him and Mr. Watson. "This gentleman is just going home."

Mr. Watson shook his head. "I suppose you're right," he sighed. He started to leave, but whirled back around still clutching his armor, and said, "Next time though, young men, be careful what you take from alleys."

Simon dodged out from behind Mom and ran over to him. "Do we have to give the beer cans back to your neighbor who's moving to Florida?" he asked. "He said we could have them. No lie."

Mr. Watson took off his hat, fanned himself with it, and chuckled. "If George MacDonald said you can have his whole junk heap, you're welcome to it. He's a real keeper, that character is, hoarded stuff for years. His wife won't let him move any of it to Florida. Go ahead and keep the cans," he said. "You're probably doing him a big favor."

"Well, good-bye, Mr. Watson. Sorry about all that," Billy said.

. "Good-bye, young men," Mr. Watson said with a little bow as he was leaving. "I will keep the naval jelly. I seem to be fresh out. Stop by for a visit and see the rest of my armor one of these days. I always like an appreciative audience. But just you stay away from my garage." And off he went. Maybe he wasn't such a bad guy after all.

The policeman put his hand on Simon's head. "Stay out of trouble now." He nodded to Mom and hurried off after Mr. Watson.

"Well, boys, are you all right now?" Mom asked.

"Sure, Mrs. Trumble, we're all right. I just wish he'd been throwing that armor away," Simon said.

"Come in if you get hungry," Mom called to us as she went back toward the house.

That left me all by myself with Billy and Simon. I didn't want to look at them. I knew Quint thought keeping the cans was a good idea. He was just trying to help me out. He's right, too, I thought. What do little kids know? They probably wouldn't even take care of those great cans. There was still time to tell them, but I couldn't do it.

"See you guys," I said, walking toward the gazebo. "I'm gonna stack cans in the castle now."

"Can we help you?" Billy asked.

"No, I want to do it," I told them. "Tomorrow you can help me put back the hammers and nails and stuff. And you can sweep up."

"Simon, do this. Billy, do that," Simon grumbled. "You want us to shine your shoes, too?" he asked.

"And brush your teeth?" Billy added. "What fun is clean-up?"

"Everything knights do for their kings isn't supposed to be fun," I explained. "Begone." I waved them away.

They gathered up their rusty punch-tops and the new beer cans, complaining all the time. And then they were gone, wagon, crummy cans, and all. Knights without armor.

7 · Taffy

Saturday was a gray, thunder-rumbling day, not at all perfect weather for Quint's block circus. Signs were taped up, anyway, on trees, lampposts, stop signs, everywhere:

CIRCUS TODAY
2 o'clock
TIGER PARADE – MAGIC – DANCING GIRLS
CLOWNS – JUGGLING – ACROBATS
at Quentin Calkins' house
1201 McCoy Street
Admission 10¢

I knew the reporter would come. The place would look great for pictures, with all the decorations, balloons, and stuff. I really wanted to go, even though Quint had been awful to me that week. I couldn't figure him out. During gym one day I told him about Mr. Watson and his armor and how he thought Billy and Simon had stolen it. I thought that would break him up, but he just said, "I bet you finally took their cans, didn't you."

"Yeah," I told him, "but I shouldn't have let you talk me into it."

61

He gave me a smirky laugh. "You're the one who did it, King Kan. I'm just a magician."

"Look, it was your idea!" I shouted. Boy, did he bug me. "You're not going to *tell* them?" I asked. And I could tell by that phony, fake smile that that was just what he was going to do. I pulled back my arm to let him have it.

"Trumble," the coach called. "Enough of that. Drop down and give me ten."

"All right. Tell them. They won't care," I told Quint and started the push-ups, which I hate. I knew they *would* care, though. I had to get to those kids somehow, before Quint did.

That's why I got to the circus early. Billy and Simon were sure to be there. Quint was using his driveway for a stage, so I sat down on the grass right at the edge of the pavement, so I'd be up front. The performers were mostly all in the garage getting ready and giggling. There were lots of little kids with clown faces painted on by their mothers and some twirlers from the Saturday morning beginner's class throwing batons up and dropping them on their heads.

I was sitting square in the middle of the front row, holding on tight to the box I'd brought with me. There was a lot of noise and yelling, so nobody noticed the squeaking and scratching inside the box.

When the popcorn kid walked by, I bought a bag for a dime, took out a big handful for me, and popped a couple of kernels into the box. I peeked inside and watched my two caramel-colored gerbils nibbling away. I had brought them as a peace offering, something to give Billy and Simon when I told them what the cans were really worth.

Lots of kids were at the circus, running around. I saw Billy and Simon. "Hey, sit down over here," I called to them. "I'll scoot over. Look, I've got something for you." I held up the box. They just stood there, not looking very friendly. "Where you been all morning?" I asked them.

"We went over to that new Hobby Hutch," Simon said slowly. "Quint told us there was something there we should see. He told us to price the beer cans there."

"He was right, too," Billy said, narrowing his eyes at me. "Mr. Grundle, the guy who owns the place, has got beer cans for sale. Not many, but enough. He's got a couple of conies like those we traded you. They cost twelve dollars each."

"It looks to us like we gave you a hundred twenty dollars worth of cans," Simon said. "Quint said you knew all the time. He said he didn't but you did."

"Yeah, Quint said the cans you gave us aren't worth a handful of beans," Billy went on. "We trusted you."

My stomach sank. The popcorn inside felt like Mexican jumping beans. I didn't know what to say. I was trapped.

"That Mr. Grundle sounds like a gyp to me," I tried. "He's asking too much. I don't know anybody who'll pay that kind of money, do you?" I said, using my dad's line. "Anyway," I smiled, weakly, "don't worry about it. It's all for the good of the king." I kept hoping they still felt a little like loyal knights. I mean, what else could I say? I was *going* to tell them. But Quint got to them first.

Just then, Quint dashed out, waving a black construction paper top hat. Somebody yelled, "Down in

front," and Simon and Billy sat down next to me on the edge of the pavement.

"Ladies and gentlemen, children of all ages," Quint shouted. "The Quentin Calkins Circus is about to begin." A bunch of little clowns came somersaulting out. Some of them did cartwheels until their hats came off, even though they were rubber-banded under their chins. They were pretty good for first-graders.

The trees were beginning to blow, the sky was filling with more gray clouds, and in the distance you could see lightning. Quint didn't seem to notice. He led a round of applause for "those great little clowns," and then introduced, "The one, the only, Quentin Calkins McCoy Street feline pet parade." We could hear thunder rumble. Quint heard it, too. "Don't worry about it," he said. "It won't rain."

Just then the reporter from the *Examiner* arrived. She was wearing jeans and a short leather jacket and she didn't look much older than a high-school kid. You could tell she was a reporter, though, because she had a camera hung around her neck and she carried a big yellow writing pad.

As soon as Quint walked off and the kids with the cats started parading in, the reporter took Quint aside and started asking him questions and writing things down.

Billy glared at me. "Did you really know what those cans were worth?" he asked.

"You can have them back," I told him.

"Then you *did* know," he said, poking Simon, who shook his head.

"I brought you guys a present," I said, trying to pretend they hadn't found me out. I could hear the gerbils scuttling around inside as I held out the box.

"MEEEEEEEEEEEEEOWOWL!" We all turned at the howl of the cat parade. A little girl in a pink ballet dress was carrying a creamy Persian, its leash wrapped around her arm. Its eyes were wild and a birthday party bow had slipped down under its chin, like a weird pink beard.

Somebody had gotten a fat kid in a cowboy suit to show two cross-eyed Siamese wearing little paper saddles, but the kid looked like he was holding wild broncos. A huge tiger cat arched his back at them, giving a deep, snakelike hiss. The fat kid started to cry. An alley cat yowled.

Last of all was a girl pushing a baby buggy. Inside, climbing out of the covers, you could see this furry jet-black creature dressed up in a frilly lace doll dress and bonnet. "Pretty kitty, pretty kitty," she kept saying to it, but no amount of "pretty kitty" was going to cool those cats down. They were mad.

Simon got up to go, tugging at Billy to come with him. "I don't like cats," he said, "and I don't like kings either. Let's get out of here."

"Simon," I called to him, "don't you guys be mad. I brought you both a present." I held up the box of gerbils.

"We don't want any presents." Billy shoved the box out of my hands so that it fell to the ground. He and Simon took off like a shot.

"WATCH OUT!" somebody screamed. I looked up and saw the Persian with the birthday bow dragging the pink ballet dancer across the grass. The cats had gone berserk.

"Where'd it come from?" somebody asked. Something brushed my hand. I looked down in the grass and saw a gerbil quivering in terror. The box was on its side and the top was off. I grabbed the poor, shaking animal, tucked him back inside his box, and started to look for the other one. I was sure he wouldn't run far.

"What is it, a rat?" somebody yelled. The cats were rioting. Owners were tugging on leashes, yelling and pulling as their cats meowed, hissed, and tug-of-warred to get away. That gerbil must have been crazy. He'd dashed straight through the legs of those cats.

Cats and kids scrambled everywhere, weaving leashes between other leashes and between legs until the driveway was a disaster area. The noise was something terrible.

Quint came running back, waving his arms. The gerbil had escaped, and all the cats seemed to have a different idea about which way he'd gone. Quint was right in the middle of it. Everybody was out of their seats laughing, trying to help, trying to unsnap leashes and tackle loose cats.

"Hey, you guys," Quint yelled. Nobody listened.

"Everybody sit down." Just then the rain started falling, big fat drops splatting on the ground. And on the
cats. The big black cat leaped angrily onto Quint's
shoulder, hissing. The reporter couldn't resist it. She
got her camera out and started snapping away. *Click*
went the camera. The kids were all running. The rain

fell harder. "Come back next Saturday and we'll do it again," Quint yelled.

Cats were everywhere. Two leashes wrapped around Quint's legs were tugged in opposite directions as kids tried to free their cats. *Click*. His feet slipped out from under him and he landed *pow* on his bottom like they do in silent movies. *Click* went the camera again.

"Here's that gerbil. I caught the gerbil," somebody called from the garage. A little kid in a wet clown suit held the gerbil up high over his head and asked, "Who's this belong to?" Nobody seemed to be paying much attention. I ran into the garage, holding tight to my box, rain dripping off the tip of my nose.

"Do you know whose gerbil this is?" the little clown asked me.

"He's mine. His name is Taffy," I told him, lifting up the lid and showing him the other gerbil. "This one's Toffee."

"Harvey Trumble did it," the kid yelled. "Hey, Quint. Harvey Trumble let the gerbil loose."

Quint ducked in the garage out of the rain. He was fuming. "I should have known it was you," he said. "You not only cheat little kids but you break up my circus. I'm gonna get you for this, Harvey Trumble!"

8 · The Royal Interview

I was sitting on my throne, waiting, when somebody knocked on the gazebo door. It was too early for the reporter, so it had to be Quint and his gang or maybe Billy and Simon with theirs, come over to bloody my nose and cauliflower my ears. I got up and looked for someplace to hide, but unless I could genie myself into a beer can there was no place to go. The knock got louder and faster.

"Harvey, Harv. You in there?" It was my brother Peter. Good old Pete.

"Enter, slave," I commanded. "Enter my castle."

"Your Majesty," he said, swinging the door open. "Your obedient servant here." He looked around the room, tracing the rainbows with his eyes. "The old gazebo will never be the same. How're you doing with all this stuff?" he asked.

"Awful," I admitted. "Being a king is great, but I'm messing everything up. Billy and Simon are mad at me because I gave them a lousy trade trying to beef up my collection. And Quint's mad. I ruined his circus yesterday." Everything, everything was wrong.

"I thought it got rained out."

"Well, I didn't make the rain, but everything else

70

was my fault. One of my gerbils got loose—accidentally, I swear—and it totaled his cat parade. Quint said he'd get me for it, too." Peter was wandering around moving cans. It didn't look like he was listening. "What do you think he'll do?" I asked Pete as I followed him, putting the cans back the way they were.

He walked over to the throne. The whole gazebo looked smaller when he was in it. He could reach up, if he wanted to, and change the lightbulb in the peak. He didn't answer my question. "Your old buddy Eric Wagner called," he told me. "He said Quint had called him. Eric said to tell you *he* knew you hadn't done anything on purpose, but that you better watch out for Quint. He's planning trouble for you."

"You mean he . . ."

"Also," he went on, "Matthew Marrinson called to ask if you were interested in trading him a Falstaff Draft for a Dixie and a Jax. His folks just brought them back from New Orleans. He said he'd decided not to enter the contest because he doesn't like to make speeches."

"That's too bad," I started, "I . . ."

"That's not all," Peter broke in. "Quint called *him*, too. Matthew wants you to know he's not going to join Quint against you."

"Against me? Did those guys say what Quint wanted them to do?" I asked him.

"Some sort of organized madness directed at you.

71

They didn't say. I didn't ask. They're your friends. Call them back and find out. Or just let it be a surprise."

He started to sit down on my throne, and was hovering about three inches over the cushion when I yelped, "Peter, don't. That throne's made of crates. You'll pulverize it."

Peter straightened up, looked for another place to sit, and, not finding one, started toward the door. "If you need any help, Harv, let me know. Though I'll admit I've never been a king's bodyguard before."

As he opened the door to take a giant step out, Julia came skipping in, beaming. "There's a lady wants to see you," she said. "She's got a camera."

"It's the reporter," I told her. "She's gonna take my picture for the paper."

Julia twirled around a few times on her toes. "Can I dress up like a princess and get my picture taken, too?" she asked.

"No, you can't," I told her, looking around to see if everything was all shaped up. "I'm the king of this place. Where is she?"

"Outside." She peeked out the door. "Talking to Peter." She turned and looked me over. "You don't look like a king," she said. "You oughta have on your crown. Where is it?"

Julia and I'd made a crown together out of old gold wrapping paper, but I thought it looked too dumb. I'd just stuck it on top of the throne. Julia saw me glance over at it and went dashing over to lift it off. "Put this on," she ordered. "It's beautiful."

I clamped the crown on my head as she dashed out the door, announcing, "My brother the king is inside the castle. That makes me a princess, you know."

The reporter patted Julia on the head and stepped in the door. She was the one who had talked to Quint. She looked around the dimly lighted gazebo. Then she saw the royal me. If she remembered me from the circus she didn't show it.

"I'm Harvey Trumble, the Beer Can King," I said, holding out my right hand and steadying my crown with my left. "I'm Karen Gray, the reporter," she said, smiling and shaking my hand. I asked her if she wanted to sit down. Since the throne was the only possible place, she said no thanks and started touring the cans.

"Where'd they all come from?" she asked me, getting her pad and pencil ready.

"Lots of places," I told her. "My uncle in Springfield got me started. He'd saved about a hundred cans and he gave them to me for my birthday three years ago. They're all mixed in with the others now because I've got them in alphabetical order." I started to lead her over to the A's, but I noticed she was writing like crazy. It scared me to watch her put my words on paper, so I stopped talking.

She stopped writing and looked up. "And you built up from there?" she said. I nodded yes. "How?" she asked. The pencil was on the paper there, ready to go. "On vacations," I said.

"On vacations," she wrote.

"Is that all?" she asked me.

"Not really," I told her. She didn't write that one down.

"You don't sound much like a king," she said, looking at my dumb crown and then at all the crazy rainbows. She started to put her pencil back in her big leather purse.

"But I really am a king," I said, pleading. "I'll tell you all about my cans. They're fantastic. Take this Rex conie, for instance," and I kept her pencil going for twenty minutes easy. I told her about cleaning up rusty cans with steel wool. I told her how to straighten out a dented can by dropping a lighted firecracker into it.

I told her about finding cans in gas station trash barrels and in alleys and dumps. I told her about snaking around on the bottom of lakes near picnic places. I told her about trades and about flea markets, about conies and punch-tops. Every time she stopped writing I told her how great I was. I even told her about my trusty knights once when I couldn't think of anything else to say. It was great being a king with an audience. I could have talked all day. I was just taking a breath to go on when she started to take out her camera.

"Hold up," she said. "I've got enough for three articles. What I need now is a picture."

I grabbed the nearest can, an old Hirshvogel quart conie, sat down on the throne, and smiled as big as I could.

Click went the camera.

"Hold the beer can up in front of you. It looks kind of old, but I guess it'll do. Up higher." *Click*. "OK, now hold the can near your face. Smile." *Click*. "I guess that's it."

"Anything else you want to know?" I asked her.

She laughed. "You know, I thought you weren't

going to talk at all there at first," she said, "but you told me all I need to know about beer cans. Thanks."

"Har-vey," Julia yelled from outside in the yard. "Harvey, you've gotta come here. Some kids are out here."

"Good old Julia," I said. "She's gotten a batch of her little friends to come and see me in my crown."

"Harvey," she yelled again. "They want to see you."

I was still seeing stars from the flashbulbs when I flung open the gazebo door. The gold paper crown sat on my head. I smiled my best, my kingliest smile— for about three seconds.

Splat. Right in the forehead it got me. Egg oozed down my eyebrows and dripped off my chin. My crown fell to the ground. *Splat.* In my hair. I wiped my eyes free of the sticky goo and saw Billy and Simon standing there, eggs in hand.

Simon was winding up.

"What's going on out . . ." *Splat.* Karen Gray got one, too.

"You guys didn't tell me you were gonna do that." Julia was crying. "That's not fair."

"Geez, I hit some lady!" Simon yelled. He and Billy dropped their eggs and took off across the grass, with me running wildly after them. They jumped over the flowers.

"Hey, King Kan," somebody called. I looked out toward the street and there was Quint, standing on

76

the sidewalk, laughing his head off.

"Some king!" he roared. He looked around, smirking, to see if any other kids were there to enjoy the mess. But I watched his face change plenty fast as his eyes reached the gazebo. The reporter was standing there, egg all over her face. She didn't see Quint. Her eyes were glued shut. But he sure saw her, and I bet he beat his own record running the hundred.

I tried running after him, but the faster I ran, the drier the egg got. My face was stuck. I couldn't move it.

When I got back, my mom was in the yard with a wet towel for the reporter. Mom was telling her what she thought of Billy and Simon. "Those boys," she was saying. "Last week, I saw them jumping up and down on the roof of the gazebo. Then, a few days later, they took somebody's valuable armor—they *said* by mistake. And now this. Well, I can't tell you how sorry I am."

Karen Gray wiped her face mostly clean with the wet towel. Then she smiled at Mom and laughed out loud when she looked me over. "You know," she said, "I thought covering this contest was going to be a real bore. But it's been incredible. Incredible," she said again, shaking her head. She was still smiling when she waved good-bye with her spattered yellow pad.

I went inside the house, filled the bathroom sink with water, and stuck my head in. As the warm water began to loosen my face, I shifted it from smile to frown and back. I puckered, blew a bubble or two, and lifted my head out of the eggy water for air. I looked in the mirror. It was pretty bad. That Billy had a good pitching arm, I'll give him that. He'd hit me square in the middle of my forehead. The hair hanging down over my eyes was all matted together

and bits of eggshell stuck in it like snowflakes. I looked more like the king's fool than the king.

Peter came in to look over the damage. "I'm not a very good bodyguard," he said. "I didn't hear a thing. You OK?"

"I'm OK. Just yucky," I told him as I soaped off the egg streams.

"Ever hear of the French Revolution?" he asked me.

"American, yes. French, no," I told him. "Don't try that high-school stuff on me."

"There was this king," he said.

"Oh, come on," I groaned. He was going to preach at me. I could tell it.

"No kidding," he said. "This kind of stuff happens to kings all the time. They get to feeling their power. They rob the peasants and the peasants get mad and fight back."

"Billy and Simon aren't peasants," I told him, as I toweled my head dry.

"I didn't say they were," he said. "Anyway, one of the reasons for this French Revolution was the king. Louis the Sixteenth. You know what they did to him?"

"I'd hate to guess."

"Guess."

"They egged him."

"Close, close," he said. "They cut off his head." He bent over the sink and chopped at his neck with the side of his hand. "Sliced it off, *thunk!*" he said, letting his head go limp.

"Oh, cut it out." I snapped the towel at him while he was bent over. He was making me mad. "Nobody's going to cut off my head for ripping off a couple of little kids."

"Aha! You admit it," he said, straightening up. "You didn't just make a good trade. You ripped them off. *That* is the downfall of kings, kid."

"Yeah, well, it just happened. Now I don't know what to do about it."

"Simple," he said. "Give them back the cans."

"Sure, simple." I wound the towel around my head like a turban. "I'll think about it."

"I would if I were you," Peter said as he left me standing there. "If you don't give those cans back pretty soon, Your Majesty," he said, "I'd bet the revolution has just begun."

9 · The Monster and the Magician

All the kids at school Monday were laughing about how I'd been egg-bombed by those two third graders. I didn't see Billy and Simon all week, though. Oh, I saw them, all right, but when they saw me they ran like crazy. I guess they thought I was really sore. But the more I thought about it, the more I was sure I would have egged the guy who cheated me out of those cans.

On Friday, Quint came up to me in the hall with two of his friends hanging around behind him. "Look," he said. "I'm gonna have another circus tomorrow and I've got some guys who are gonna be there looking for you. Not just Billy and Simon this time, either. I've got more." The warning bell rang and everybody started slamming lockers and running toward their rooms.

"I don't care about your old circus," I said.

"You better not come, that's all," he told me. "You better not." And he ran off down the hall.

I decided right then to go, but I wasn't exactly sure how. I couldn't see getting together a gang of guys to force my way in. I didn't want to ruin the dumb circus again. Anyway, Julia was going to be in it this

81

time, wearing her new tutu, and she'd kill me if I botched it up for her. There had to be some secret way to go.

Julia woke me up on Saturday morning. "Mom's gone shopping," she said. "You've got to fix your own breakfast. And we're out of peanut butter." She handed me a sheet of paper that had been printed on some kid's printing press.

QUENTIN CALKINS CIRCUS
FABULOUS JUGGLING AND MAGIC SHOW
today at 2
Absolutely free to Kids who paid last week
Absolutely one dime to Kids who didn't
NO CAT PARADE

Julia said a couple of girls were handing out the ads on Lake Street.

"You gonna come and see me do the splits?" Julia asked.

"I don't know," I told her. "Go away and let me wake up." I got up, washed my face awake and tried to start thinking about disguises.

First, I decided on clown makeup. But I figured somebody would be sure to find out it was me under the paint. Then I wandered into Pete's room to look at his mask collection. Most of them were stashed away in his closet, but three of them were sitting on stands on his dresser. There was his Richard Nixon mask. It was a great one. It really was. But it wouldn't do. I used it once for Halloween and people kept stopping me and asking me questions. People want to talk to Richard Nixon. The ape mask was pretty good, but it was new last year, so I decided to wear Pete's old monster mask. It was horrible, green-gray and yellow soft rubber, with pink scars and two gruesome fangs. Nobody would even see my hair because the mask covered my whole head. Next to it on the dresser were ugly, warty monster hands with long jagged green claws. They were perfect. Nobody would even notice me, I would look so circus in a getup like that. Nobody was likely to come up and ask a monster questions, either.

But the beer cans were another problem. Somehow, I had to get those conies back to Billy and Simon. Those ten cans were driving me batty. I just wasn't sure how to return them. Should I stack them up on one of their porches and let it go at that? Should I wrap them up like presents and drop them down their chimneys? Maybe I could just walk right up and say something sincere like, "Here you are, my friends. I am deeply, deeply sorry. I have decided I was wrong wrong and you were right right and you can keep your stupid cans."

Actually, I tried out several speeches, but I could always imagine Billy shouting out something like, "Couldn't take the eggs, could you? What's the matter, scared?" when it really wasn't that at all. I just felt guilty. I tried to tell myself that we *did* shake on the trade, after all. I *did* give them some of my cans for theirs. It wasn't as if I stole them. But I couldn't talk myself into it. I'd given them a crummy trade and that was that.

I went out to the gazebo, unlocked the door, turned on the light, and looked around. It was still a great castle. Those ten beautiful conies were lined up on a stack of boards we'd painted with the leftover gold. I'd buffed off the bad rust with steel wool, shined them up with naval jelly, and coated them with wax, so they looked first-rate.

I wrapped each can carefully in a sheet of newspaper and put them all in a big grocery bag. I figured I'd think of some way to deliver them to Billy and Simon.

At two o'clock I left for Quint's circus with my big bag of cans. My hands and face were all sweaty inside the monster getup and my hair was sticking to my forehead, but I figured if Pete could take it on Halloween, I could stand it for an hour or so.

On a lamppost down the street there was a poster that said Eric Wagner was going to give a skateboard show at four o'clock on Suicide Hill. That meant Karen Gray would be at it again, taking pictures and asking questions. After the circus I'd go over and watch him. Suicide Hill's no joke. It's really steep, heading down toward the creek and the bandshell in the park. But Eric's good . . . wears elbow and knee pads both. He sure makes that board work for him.

Wandering into Quint's driveway, I passed the kid who was collecting dimes, waved my green claws at her, and walked on in. She waved back and giggled at me.

The little clowns were already somersaulting. I had this creepy feeling that I'd done all this before and that it wasn't going to be any fun at all. Billy and Simon were in front with a gang of kids, eating popcorn and shouting to a tiny clown in a pointed hat, "Stand on your point, pencil head."

I leaned up against the tree, back from the crowd, and put the bag of cans down next to me. A little kid selling popcorn edged cautiously over to me. I bought some from him with the dime I had in my paw. I'd brought it along just in case I had to pay to get in.

It's very hard to get popcorn out of a bag when you're wearing warty rubber hands and it's even harder to fit it in the mouth slit of a mask. I tried. I even got some inside, but the mouth of the mask was about an inch below my chin. The popcorn just kept slipping out of the mask and into my shirt. It was useless.

Giving up, I looked over to see Quint running in to announce, "And now, ladies and gentlemen, it's time for MAGIC!" He flung out his hands and, suddenly, a very long black cane with a white tip appeared in one of them. Just like that. It really wasn't there before. He twirled it around, stuck it under his arm, and bowed. The kids all clapped. It was pretty good. I clapped, too.

Next, Quint called up one of Julia's friends, a little kid in a blue ballet dress and a pink feather thing in her hair. She was pretty nervous with everybody looking at her, but she managed to crumble a soda cracker Quint gave her into a metal pan, just like he asked her to. Then he handed her a jack of diamonds and asked her to tear it in half.

"*Tear* it?" she asked. She couldn't believe he really wanted her to.

"Sure, tear it in half," he said.

She tore it in four pieces. He took the torn-up card and tossed it in the pan with the cracker crumbs, put a lid on the pan and waved his cane around going "Presto-chango" and "Hocus pocus dominocus." He told her to close her eyes and blow her magic breath on the pan. She did it, and you could tell she believed she was really working a spell, too. She opened her eyes. Quint lifted the lid off, and—you're not going to believe this—but right there where the crackers and the torn jack had been, there was this big box of Cracker Jacks.

"Cracker—Jacks!" Quint said. "Get it?" Everybody had already gotten it. And they clapped a lot. I clapped with my rubber mitts. I was feeling kind of hot inside, but this was fun. I was glad I'd come.

Then Quint held his hands up to quiet everybody and said, "I need another helper."

All the kids in front were waving their hands in the air, screaming, "Me! Me! My turn!" Quint roamed his eyes over the group in front of him. He glanced over at me, leaning against the tree, looked away, and then looked quickly back again.

"I want the monster," he said slowly.

All the kids stopped yelling "Me! Me!" and turned around to see what he was talking about. They must have figured this was all set up ahead of time because a couple of guys in clown suits started to shout, "We want the monster."

I shook my head no.

Quint nodded his head yes, and everybody laughed. I couldn't tell if he knew who I was or not. "This trick is perfect for the monster," he said with a mean grin. And I decided he knew. Somehow, he could tell.

Everybody started chanting, "We want the *mon*-ster. We want the *mon*-ster." Some little kids ran up and started pushing at the backs of my knees, moving me forward. I kept shaking my head no and they kept yelling *"Mon*-ster."

The cans! When I turned back to get them they were almost out of reach. I lunged back, grabbed the sack, and let myself be swept along in a tide of little kids, right up to Quint.

When everybody had settled down, Quint held up

an old *Examiner* with a picture of a burning grocery store on the front page.

"Now, everybody remember this page," he said. "Find something on it you'll recognize when you see it again." Then he turned to me. "All I want you to do is tear this newspaper in half. Can you tear paper absolutely straight, monster?"

I shook my head no, wiggling my rubber claws. The crowd giggled.

"Then I'll do it myself," he said. He held the newspaper up high and tore it in half the long way. Next he tore each of those pieces into two strips. Because I was standing so close, I could step a little behind him. I could see another newspaper. It was folded and pasted on the back of one of the torn strips. Seeing that, it wasn't hard to figure out how the trick was done. He was going to fold up the pieces and open up that other paper. It would look like the first one had just magicked itself back together.

"This is some rip-off, isn't it?" Quint said, getting another laugh, as he tore the newspaper into more pieces.

Rip-off? That's why he called me up here. That's why he said it would be a good trick for the monster. He was going to say something about me and that other rip-off.

In the front row Billy and Simon were laughing. Simon was pointing at the newspaper and talking all excited about something. I tried to listen. I could hear Simon say he'd figured out how the trick worked. Maybe he'd seen the folded-up paper, too.

I looked back at Quint just as he was presto- changoing. He folded up the torn pieces into a small package and suddenly, *flip*, there was one whole newspaper with a picture of a burning grocery store on the front page.

Everybody yelled and shouted and I could hear Simon saying, "See, see, I told you so."

Quint got everybody quiet and started off with, "That was some rip-off. Didn't I tell you? And now," he said, "for yet another rip-off." I could feel his hand grab the back of my mask. "Hold still," he said, quietly. He was getting ready to tear it off with everybody watching.

I had to do something. I couldn't run or disappear. Fighting him would break up the circus again. The kids were all watching close. They thought it was just part of the act, The Monster and the Magician. I decided to keep the act going.

Just as Quint was yanking the mask up in back, I raised my claws up high and roared. It was a ferocious, monster roar—loud, but muffled and mysterious, since the mask kept part of it echoing inside. Everybody stopped talking. Quint dropped his hand and stepped back.

"A prize," I roared. "I have a prize." I held up the beer-can bag and swung it back and forth in front of them. "The Monster will give a rich prize to the

first person who can tell how the Magician performed his fantastic newspaper trick."

Simon jumped to his feet. "I can!" he shouted. A lot of other kids shouted, "Me," but I pointed a claw at Simon. "I can," he said again. "He had another newspaper folded up and pasted on the back! Right?"

"You're right," I growled as loud as I could. "You've guessed the Magician's deepest hidden secret." I bowed and pointed to Quint, who didn't bow, and everybody cheered. This, I decided, was the time to leave. The kids were yelling, "*mon*-ster, *mon*-ster," as I waved good-bye. I tossed the bag of cans to Simon, yelled, "The Monster congratulates you on your all-seeing eyes," and growled off down the driveway. Quint was standing there with his mouth open, not knowing what to do. I guess the only thing he could do was go on with the next act, Julia and her friends in tutus doing the splits, maybe.

Sweat had collected in my ears and my hair was as wet as if I'd been swimming. When I took off the mask a block or so away I must have looked like an endangered seal. I sure felt like one. I had to laugh, though. What if Quint had torn off the mask and it was some other kid, not me at all? I whistled as I walked along.

"Harvey?" a voice said. I turned around. It was Suzanna, tooling along on her unicycle. "You all right?" she asked. "You look funny."

"I'm great," I told her. "I'm just sweating from this monster mask." I held it up for her to see and she looked at me as though I was absolutely off my rocker.

"Hey, Harvey! Harv!" Suzanna and I both turned this time. Billy and Simon were running down the street, shouting.

91

"You were really great, Harv," Billy yelled. "You really were funny."

"We didn't know it was you until we opened the bag. No lie. But you didn't need to give back the beer cans," Simon said. "We were just mad that you traded like that." He held out the bag. "We didn't really want the cans."

"I don't want them either," I told them, putting my hands behind my back. "They're yours. You found them. Every time I see them they give me the creeps."

"Take them," Simon said.

"I can't," I said again.

"Beer cans?" Suzanna asked, getting off her unicycle. "Good ones?"

"Conies," I told her, figuring she wouldn't have any idea what I was saying.

"You're kidding," she said. "I'll take them if neither of you wants them."

"What for?" Simon asked.

"What do you mean, what for?" Suzanna asked. "For collecting, of course. What else would you do with conies?"

"You've got a collection?" I asked her, wondering if she was putting me on.

"Sure, I've got a collection," she said. "Well, really, my dad and I have this collection. He drives a truck and he picks them up from all over the country. And when he's home sometimes we go out looking for cans. Then we blast out the dents or fill them with water and freeze them out. We clean and buff and wax them, you know, stuff like that. We've got one thousand, one hundred and forty-eight cans from all over, and we're going to a collectors' convention this summer while Dad's on vacation."

I crumpled the mask up and stuck it in my pocket. "A thousand one hundred forty-eight? You really mean it?" I asked her. "Lots of doubles?"

"Not counting doubles," Suzanna said. "Dad says it's not fair to count doubles." I was beginning to sweat as bad as when I had the mask on. I rubbed the drops off my forehead with my sleeve.

"Look, I know what these cans are worth," Suzanna said. "Nobody's going to give them away." She laughed.

"It's OK with us," Simon said.

"Take them," I told her. "You and your dad can have them." They had a *lot* more than me. They made my collection look like zero, zilch.

"Look," Suzanna said, "my dad won't be back in town until Tuesday, but I'll take these home and see what he says. Thanks a lot." She hopped back on her unicycle, circling around a couple of times before she rode off, holding the bag of conies in one hand and waving good-bye with the other.

A thousand one hundred and forty-eight cans! Some Beer Can King I was turning out to be.

10 · The Boy Who Would Be King

I had tons of homework Monday. I was sitting in front of the TV watching a game show and trying to figure out how you're supposed to divide decimals when Julia called me.

"Harvey," she yelled. "Har-vey, come here."

I didn't answer. If I came every time Julia called me, that's all I'd have time to do.

"Harvey," she called again. "Come here!"

On the other hand, if I didn't answer, she'd keep calling me forever.

"I'm busy," I said, thinking that might do it. I tried to remember whether you move the decimal point right or left.

"Harvey!" She was mad now. "Don't you *care* that your picture's in the paper?"

That did it. I got downstairs by the bannister in three seconds flat. She didn't even try to hide the paper from me. I grabbed it and lay back on the living-room sofa to soak in the glory.

"SUPERKIDS FINALISTS," the headline said. Underneath were six pictures and mine was one of them. The girls were Anne Wilson, this kid who swims like a salmon, Debby Goldsmith, who plays a mean flute, and Suzanna Brooks. There was a really great photo of her eating a hamburger while she rode on her unicycle.

The boys were Quint, Eric Wagner, and me! Quint's picture was the funniest. It was the one Karen Gray took when the cats were starting to tie knots around his legs. The black cat in a dress was clinging to his shoulder and he looked like his face was about to slide off. Under the picture in big letters it said, "The Presto Chango Kid." I skimmed the article, which told mostly how hard he practiced his magic and how the little children of the neighborhood adored him for putting on magic shows for them.

Eric Wagner's picture was a good one. He was standing on his head on his skateboard, smiling. You had to turn the picture upside down to see the smile. From the way he looked, you knew he could skateboard down roller-coaster tracks if he wanted to. Under his picture it said, "Down the Hill Upside Down."

Then there was me. It was a dumb picture. My old Hirshvogel can was stuck out toward the camera in perfect focus. Behind it, kind of hazy in the background, was me in my crown. The gold wrapping had peeled down from its points and you could see the cardboard underneath as plain as day. I had a silly grin on my face, too. It wasn't the picture I'd thought it would be. One thing it *didn't* look was grand and noble. But under the photo was the real clincher, like a big put-down. It said, "The Boy Who Would Be King."

I didn't want to read any farther, but I couldn't help myself. "Harvey Trumble," it said, "wants to be a king. He even has a castle. It's a boarded-up, wildly painted gazebo in his backyard. The boards are there to keep the rain from blowing in and the paint forms vivid psychedelic rainbows inside. At the end of each rainbow is Harvey Trumble's treasure, beer cans.

"Harvey has a big collection of beer cans stacked all around his castle, which he decorated with the help of two neighbor boys he calls his 'trusty knights,' Billy Leonard and Simon Kelly. 'They're little kids who like to work for me,' Harveys says."

I groaned out loud. I couldn't believe I had said that. But I remembered how much I wanted to keep Karen Gray interested during that interview. I could have said anything. Billy and Simon are going to explode, I thought. It's going to be worse than eggs this time.

" 'A lot of my cans are really rare,' " the article went on. It hurt my head to read it, but I couldn't stop. " 'I have a fabulous collection,' Harvey points out. The cans in his gazebo have such names as Royal Bohemian, Regal, and Rex. 'I really had to work hard to find great ones like that,' Harvey told me."

"Good grief," I moaned. Those were the cans I got from Billy and Simon. They were the cans we'd given

Suzanna. And there I was in the paper, big-dealing about how hard *I'd* worked to get them. I considered crawling under the front porch and staying there a week or two. But I read on.

" 'I'm fantastic at this,' the eleven-year-old collector said, leaning back in his gilded grapefruit-crate throne."

"Not eleven, *twelve!*" I shouted. "I'm twelve. Can't she get anything right?"

" 'And I bet I've got more cans than anybody in town.' Harvey has 'somewhere between six and seven hundred good ones.' He thinks it's the best hobby there is because 'I help keep the world clean by picking up junk.' If he keeps going, Harvey Trumble could well become a Beer Can King."

Right now, I thought, people all over Pittsfield are reading this article and they're laughing like crazy. All except Billy and Simon, and they're not laughing at all. I could just imagine what it would be like when Suzanna's dad got back in town and saw how many cans I thought was a stupendous collection.

That article was like one of those magazine stories you read about movie stars and you just know you wouldn't like them if you met them. Only it was about *me*. And all the things I didn't like the most were in quotation marks. It was me that said them.

"Harvey," Peter yelled. "Somebody wants to talk to you on the telephone."

"I'm busy," I told him. I didn't want to hear what anybody had to say. "Take a message."

I waited, thinking it couldn't be anything good. Pete stuck his head in the living room. "It was Mr. Grundle," he said, "the guy who owns that new Hobby Hutch. He wonders if you'd stop by and see him. He'd like to talk to you about beer cans." Pete looked over my shoulder and saw my picture. "Hey, that's you, kid. Congratulations," he said, lifting the paper out of my hands.

As quick as I could, I got out of there. I decided I might as well go over and see what Mr. Grundle wanted. I'd only been in his place once and it didn't look half bad.

I took the skateboard, whizzing along past everybody. I didn't stop once, except at curbs.

Mr. Grundle was in, and about ten little kids were milling around the train that he'd set up in the middle of the store. They were poking at things, but nobody was buying. Mr. Grundle looked up from the train display.

"Why, Harvey," he said, "you sure got here in a hurry. Did your mother drive you?"

"No," I told him. "I rode my skateboard. How'd you know I was Harvey?"

"I saw your picture in the paper," he said. "It said you know a lot about cans. And I don't. I bought this collection from my cousin. He said it might bring kids into the store. But cans take up too much space. I'm just going to see if I can sell what I have here.

I don't plan to get any more." He looked up at the shelf of cans and shook his head. "The trouble is I don't know how to price these. I thought maybe you could help me. The prices my cousin said I should charge are just too high. No kid's going to pay twelve dollars for a can."

"Don't price them too low, either," I warned him. "I can help you out some, but Suzanna Brooks and her father have got a much bigger collection than I do and they go to beer-can conventions and everything. They can give you better advice than I can."

"I thought you had the biggest collection in town," Mr. Grundle said, kind of surprised.

"So did I," I told him.

Mr. Grundle turned away to help this little kid who wanted to buy a Pearl beer can that was up on the shelf. "What do you think, Harvey?" he asked me. "How much?"

I looked it over. "It's got a scratch on it," I told him. "I'd give it to her for a quarter."

"Twenty-five cents, young lady," he said. The kid seemed pretty pleased, and I asked her how many cans she had at home.

"Forty-three," she told me. "This one makes forty-four."

I turned to Mr. Grundle. "So you don't want to buy my cans?" I asked him.

"Buy them?" He hadn't expected that. "Why do you want to sell them?"

"Oh, I don't know," I shrugged. I started to say

that I'd found out somebody else had more, but that sounded stupid. Because I'd made a dumb trade? That didn't sound like a good reason either. "I don't know," was all I could think of.

"There are a lot of kids come in here wanting to trade beer cans with me," he said, nodding toward his beer-can display. "Why don't you start a club, Harvey? You could get all the collectors together so they could trade with each other. You could make lists of what everybody's got and what they want to trade. I think they'd like that a lot. Maybe you could even build your collection that way." He walked over and told some little kid not to take the train off the track.

"I'll think about that," I called to him. "I really will. But you better talk to the Brookses about the prices. Thanks a lot, Mr. Grundle."

I was feeling better when I swung open the door to walk out. He'd really wanted my advice on beer cans. But standing right out in front, eating cherry snow cones, were Billy, Simon, and a couple of their friends. I got goosebumps on my neck imagining what a cherry snow cone would feel like melting down my spine.

"Well," Simon said, "if it isn't the King Kan Monster. Want some snow cone, King?" He grinned and faked a big windup with his cone.

"You must have seen the paper," I said.

"Yeah," Billy answered. "My mother said it sounded like we were your slaves or something."

"I didn't say it like that," I said. "The reporter got it all wrong. Maybe she said that stuff because you got her in the face with an egg. Think what your mom would have said if *that* had got in the paper." It was probably hitting below the belt to get them with that, but it worked. Even Simon didn't know what to say.

"Anyway, we're making signs for Eric Wagner," Billy said. "They say, 'Wagner's a Superskate.'"

"That's not fair," I said. "You can't even vote. You're not in the sixth grade."

"We can't vote, but we can make signs if we wan to," Billy said. "We watched him go down Suicid Hill doing stunts. He's a pro."

Just then, Quint rode up at full speed on his bik When he braked he left a skid line a meter lon "Well," he said, "I see you guys are getting the tru about beer cans from 'The Boy Who Would King.'"

"Sure," I said, "why not? And how's the Kid w the Cat on his Neck?"

"Ah, that's not the question," he said. "The q tion is, 'How's the guy on the skateboard?' Did hear?"

"No," I said. "Hear what?"

"Eric Wagner was skateboarding right-side-up d his driveway after school. He hit this crack crashed. His brother says he's at the hospital a broken collarbone." He smiled that smirky s "We may be the only two guys running tomo

Monster. Just me and the Beer Can Cheat. And just wait'll you hear what I say about you in my speech."

He got on his bike and sped away.

11 · X Marks the Ballot

The day of the contest it was raining. It was kind of dark and you could see the lights in the classrooms from three blocks away. I stood for a minute outside school with the water running off my yellow poncho, wondering if I should go back home and say I was sick. I looked up at the *1948* cast in concrete in the arch over the big front door. It was right below my homeroom on the second floor, and there were already kids standing by the window at the pencil sharpener. The school bus was pulling up, bringing kids in from the country, and the rain was coming down harder, so I decided to go in.

I chucked the poncho in my locker. In the hall there were lots of notebook-paper signs written with felt-tip pens. Stuff like "Suzanna Brooks Is Super Great. She's So Fast She's Never Late." And "Anne Wilson, Swimmer—Is a Winner." Some of them had rhymes that would make you gag. I saw one of the circus kids with a "De-Throne King Kan. Quint's Our Man" sign that sounded like Quint had written it. There was a "Harvey Drinks" sign. I tore it down and crumpled it up.

"Hey, Harv," somebody called. I looked around

and saw Tom Andrews, Matt Marrinson, and a couple of other kids hanging around the new trophy case in the front hall. It had this big sheet of glass in front, a couple of empty shelves, and an overhead light that wasn't plugged in yet. It had real possibilities. Down on his knees, in front of it, the janitor was hammering a little brass plate on the bottom edge of the case.

"How's it going?" Matt asked me.

"It's going great," I lied. "What's that thing say?"

"Just some junk about the *Examiner* donating it," he said, shrugging.

"This'll really be a good place for Field Day trophies, no joke," Tom was telling somebody. "Our homeroom got one for high points last spring and then they kept the thing in the principal's office all year long."

"He didn't run anything but the stopwatch. Why should he get to keep it?" Matt turned around to me. "Your name gonna be on one of the first two trophies in here, Harv?"

"Sure," I told him. "Sure it is. If you guys vote for me."

"Count on me," Matt said.

"Yeah, well, see you around, Harv," Tom muttered and wandered off.

I could tell I was going to have to stir up some votes, so I walked on down the hall with a politician's smile, saying hello to everybody, even the girls all clustered around their lockers.

Billy and Simon were taping up one of their "Eric Wagner, Superskate" posters next to the gym.

"Hey, you guys," I called. "I talked to Eric's mother last night on the phone. She says he's gotta be in the hospital a couple of days."

Quint came rushing up and tried to shoulder me away. "I don't see how you little kids can put up posters for Eric after all I've done for you," he said. "Besides, he's not running anymore."

"Isn't Eric gonna be in the contest?" Billy asked.

"It's not fair if he can't," Simon said.

"There's nothing in the rules that says he has to be here," I said, trying to remember what the rules said.

"That shows how much you know. I just read the rules again," Quint announced. "They say that the sixth-graders vote after they've heard the finalists speak. I say that unless Eric is on the stage this afternoon, he's not in the contest. That's what I say."

"Quentin Calkins, you're a creep," I growled. "I'm gonna see to it that you lose this contest."

Quint laughed. "Look who's talking," he said as loud as he could. He tried to get the kids walking down the hall to listen to him. "This kid who cheats third-graders when he's trading beer cans . . ."

"He's not all that bad," Simon cut in.

"Besides, we're big enough to take care of ourselves," Billy added.

"He cheats little kids," Quint shouted on, unstoppable, "breaks up my circus . . ." Kids started hanging around to listen, hoping, I guess, for a fight.

"The rain did that," I said.

"Cheats little kids, breaks up my circus, brags like a fool in the paper about a really nothing beer-can collection . . ."

I couldn't think of anything to say to that one. It was true.

"And King Kan says he's gonna see to it that *I* don't win this contest. You're not going to have anybody voting for you, buddy. So you're not going to keep me from doing anything. All I've got to do is give my talk, read the rules about how the finalists have to give speeches, and it's you against me. After I say a few choice things about you, I give you one guess who gets his name engraved on a trophy."

"I may not win," I told him, trying to stare him down, "but you won't either."

"You sound pretty sure of yourself," Quint said as he strolled off down the hall. "What'd you do? Bring your handy-dandy gerbils to school with you?"

"I don't like Quint anymore," Simon said, picking up his books.

"Me neither," Billy agreed.

"Yeah," I said, "but you're not voting this afternoon. I've gotta think of something to do. I may not be so great, but he's the least Superkid I know." And I hurried off down the hall.

Suzanna was walking along with a gang of girls,

some of them waving Suzanna signs. "We're voting for you, Harvey," Suzanna called to me.

"I'm not," said one of the other girls.

"Well, I am," Suzanna announced. "See you later, Harv."

I sat down on the bench where the kids wait to go into the office, under the big picture of George Washington. I had to figure out what I was going to do. Quint was going around calling me a bragger and a cheat. The circus kids were still mad, and I couldn't prove I didn't let my gerbil go on purpose. I was just sitting there looking at nothing, waiting for some bright idea, when the principal, Mr. Healy, tapped me on the shoulder and said, "Did somebody send you to the office, Harvey?"

Mr. Healy's way over six feet and he towered over me, looking grim. I could tell he didn't know whether to be nice to me or treat me like I had just been caught dropping a water balloon out the window.

"No, no, sir," I said, jumping up. "Just resting."

"Getting ready for your big talk this afternoon? Well, now, I expect you'd like to have a big case like our new one to display your collection, wouldn't you?" he asked. His little brown moustache twitched.

"Oh, sure, yes, I would." The bell rang, so I picked up my books and headed upstairs toward homeroom.

At two o'clock all the fourth-, fifth-, and sixth-graders filed into the auditorium for the assembly to hear the finalists. Since Eric was still in the hospital, there were just five of us kids on the stage. The foot-lights were on and we couldn't see much on the other side of them. You could sure hear all those kids, though. It sounded like a waterfall.

I had a speech written down on three-by-five cards. I'd written it the night before. It was about beer cans. I hadn't known what to say, so I put down what my dad suggested—stuff from a book, mostly, about the history of beer cans. Ho, hum. That's ten votes right there, I figured—the teachers and Mr. Healy. Except they can't vote. I folded the cards up, stuck them in my back pocket, and started to panic.

Everybody got quiet. A couple of Girl Scouts led the Pledge, and we all sang "America the Beautiful." Then the fourth-grade chorus lined up in front of the stage and got through "This Land is Your Land" and something else I forgot to listen to. Before I knew it, Mr. Healy bounded up the stage steps, stood at the microphone, and raised it about four feet. I blinked, trying to see past the footlights.

"Boys and girls," he said. You could hear his voice booming over the PA system. "This is a special day for Central School. Today we are receiving a very useful and decorative gift from the Pittsfield *Examiner*. How many of you have seen the new display case in the front hall?"

Everybody raised their hands. I mean, you couldn't have missed it, really. It was right out there.

"Now," he went on, "I knew that all of the children involved in competing for trophies on Field Day—

all the fourth-, fifth-, and sixth-graders—would espe-
cially want to be here to express their thanks. People,
I want you to give our very finest welcome to the man
who is responsible for giving us such a fine present—
the president of our local Lions Club, Editor-in-Chief
of the *Examiner*, and our good friend, Mr. George
Adams."

They clapped pretty hard, and I expect Mr. Adams
felt good about the whole thing because, after he low-
ered the mike, he talked on and on about how everyone in this fine auditorium is a good sport and a super
kid and how he'd thought about this whole thing
one day when he saw the trophies sitting on a shelf
in the principal's office. Then he held up these two
gold cups and said everybody deserved them but that
he was certainly looking forward to the speeches of
the fine young people who were the finalists.

I wasn't, but I was glad, anyway, when he sat down.

The girls talked first. The first two told about how
great they were at home, at school, at play, in the
community, in the nation, in the world, in the uni-
verse. Boy, was I getting bored. Suzanna was different.
She unicycled up to the front of the stage and got
a big hand. She gave her whole talk, which was short,
while she rode on the unicycle. She didn't even use
the microphone. Everybody liked it. Mr. Adams was
smiling his head off. You could tell he thought those
girls were "fine young people."

Quint was next. He was nervous. While everybody
talked, he'd been bending his cards back and forth,

and they were a mess. I guess he must not have realized it because when he held them up to read from them, he looked pretty shocked.

"Fellow sixth-graders," he said, "and all you fourth- and fifth-graders, too." Then he turned around and looked at me with that big phony smile. "I guess Harvey Trumble and me are the only two boys running in this contest."

You could hear a murmur out in the auditorium. The kids must have wondered what he was up to. "Last night I read the rules for this contest again," he went on, "and they say . . ." He shuffled through his cards, found the one he wanted, and started to read from it. " 'The winners will be chosen by a vote of the Central School sixth-graders on Tuesday, May 18, after an assembly at which the finalists will speak.' That means that since Eric can't speak at this assembly, he can't be in the contest."

The buzz in the audience got louder. Mr. Adams frowned and leaned over to talk to Mr. Healy, so I don't think they heard Quint when he said, "You should vote for me instead of Harvey because he cheats when he trades cans from his little collection, because . . ." The audience was really rumbling by then. I grabbed hold of the edge of my chair. I couldn't let him get away with that. Some guys in front were booing and I could see my homeroom teacher, Mrs. Faris, stand up and try to quiet the class. Even Quint could tell he'd gone too far. He suddenly started talking fast about his back-yard circus and his community spirit, but the mumbling went on.

Mr. Healy stood up. "All right, people!" he boomed. "I don't want to have to talk to you about rude behavior today. Give Quentin your attention."

As soon as Mr. Healy sat down, Quint threw his hands out wide and the long black cane appeared in one of them, just like it did at his circus. It was still a good trick and got a laugh.

"So," he shouted into the mike, "now that you know who to vote for . . ." He drew a big fake gun out of his pocket. "I'm going to leave you with a . . ." He pointed the gun offstage, Mr. Healy got an anxious look on his face, and everybody waited for some kind of explosion. But when he pulled the trigger a flag dropped down. *BANG*, it said. A lot of kids laughed. Some of them clapped. Quint bowed like a magician and sat down. The question was, were they clapping for him or his tricks?

It was my turn. My hands were just pouring sweat and I wasn't sure my knees would make it to the microphone. I put my cards on the stand and looked out. At the microphone I could finally see all those kids staring up at me. I glanced back down at the cards. "I am very proud to be a finalist in this contest," I read, realizing all along that I was saying each word separate—like little kids read. I wiped my palms on the seat of my jeans and looked up again. "I collect beer cans," I said.

"He collects gerbils, too." I heard a girl giggle.

111

I looked around at Quint and saw him grinning. Mrs. Faris said, "Shush."

"Well, anyway." I went on reading my cards. "I found out in a book about beer cans that they started manufacturing them in 1935 and that now there are a quarter of a million beer-can collectors in this country. First, they were made of . . . of . . ." I lost my place and squinted at my cards. The lights were hot, and it felt like a hundred degrees. My hands were still sweating and my throat was dry as sand. I could feel the panic building up again.

Quint coughed. I could hear him behind me. The kids were really restless, talking and shuffling their feet. I looked down again and opened my mouth. Nothing came out. Then, all of a sudden, the cards slipped through my hands and fell on the floor. They scattered all over, and one or two even fell off the stage. Quint broke up. The kids roared, all of them. It went on forever. I wanted to go back to the gazebo.

I picked the cards up, one by one, but it was hopeless. I'd never find my place again. It was all over for me. Eric sure was one lucky kid not having to stand up here and talk. I'd rather bust my shoulder any old day. Anyway, I thought, it was stupid that Eric couldn't win.

Then it dawned on me that it was *too* stupid, that I could *make* him win if I wanted to. I wouldn't get a trophy, but I could keep Quint from walking off with one.

I just stood there waiting, not feeling like I was in a steam bath anymore. Finally, the kids stopped laughing. I guess they were wondering what I'd say next.

I held onto the stand and leaned over to the microphone. "Listen, I've got a good idea. Instead of voting for me, maybe you should vote for Eric Wagner. The

only reason he's not here is that he's in the hospital with a broken collarbone." There were a few whispers, but then it got very, very quiet. They were listening.

"I'll speak for Eric," I said—slow, because I wasn't sure what to say next. "He's a real pro on the skateboard. And a nice guy. And I don't see any reason why a bad accident like he had should keep him from winning the contest, do you?" I turned around to look at Quint. He was green.

There was a lot of clapping. They liked it. Somehow, I'd said the right thing. I didn't know whether to be happy or sick. Then they stopped clapping and waited again.

"I want to take this opportunity," I went on, trying to sound official instead of defeated, "to say that anybody who'd like to belong to a beer-can collectors' club should meet me—in front of the Hobby Hutch this afternoon—at three-thirty." I looked down, grabbed my unused cards, and mumbled, ". . . and maybe I can be president of that."

When I sat down there was a lot of talking and some more clapping and Quint leaned over and said, "Harvey Trumble, you are a rat, a sneaky rotten rat."

"Thanks," I said, and smiled out at the audience.

Mr. Healy walked over to the mike. "Boys and girls," he said. Nothing happened. "All right, now, people. I know this is an exciting time for you, but I'd like your attention. Mr. Adams and I have been talking." He glanced over to Mr. Adams, who nodded. "And we feel that while it may be *strictly* true, according to the rules, that Eric should be here in order to qualify, we know you all agree that our good sportsmanship should allow Eric to be a contestant. You were right about that, Harvey," he said, and smiled at me.

"So, if the teachers will please pass out ballots to the sixth-graders, they may vote. Mark an X by the name of one boy and one girl."

They even passed out ballots on the stage. I couldn't help it. I voted for myself. And for Suzanna.

While they counted the votes, we had to sing. I guess it was to keep us from talking. Before they finished adding them up we'd gotten through "On Top of Old Smoky," which almost everybody sings "On Top of Spaghetti," and then a couple of rounds of "Row, Row, Row Your Boat" which the little kids always turn into "Propel, Propel, Propel Your Craft." I don't know why it should take so long to count ninety-three ballots.

Mr. Adams made the announcement. He stepped up to the mike carrying the trophies and a piece of paper. "The results are in," he said, beaming. "These two trophies go into Nielsen's Jewelers this very afternoon to have names engraved on them, names of the two sixth-graders you have chosen to be winners of our Superkids Contest." Then he paused, just to make us wait. "And *then* the trophies will be placed in the

115

brand new trophy case." He paused again, and you could tell then that he was playing this kind of game with us, dangling us along, that he still wasn't going to announce it right away. "And *then* after next week's Field Day, there'll be even more awards for the glass case." He waited again, liking all that suspense. Kids began to giggle. "Well, I guess it's time to announce the winners. It gives me great personal pleasure to introduce the young lady who received the most votes, an *Examiner* paper carrier—Miss Suzanna Brooks. Let's have a nice hand for Suzanna." Suzanna stood up and gave a little wave to the audience.

"Way to go, Suzanna!" somebody yelled.

"And the young man who won—is going to be mighty happy to hear about this in his hospital bed. It's Eric Wagner."

And that was that. I don't know whether I did the right thing or not. I felt kind of noble, telling everybody they should vote for a sick kid in the hospital. That was *very* nice of me, I thought. I honestly did feel like a good guy. I even wondered once or twice why somebody as good as I am wasn't elected Superkid after all.

12 · Hirshvogel

I got to the Hobby Hutch as soon as I could, around
3:25. The rain had stopped, but there were lots of
puddles in the street. A crowd of kids had gathered.
Some of them were talking about the contest. "Hey,
Harv," one guy said, "you should have stuck in there.
Maybe you'd have won." Maybe. Maybe I would
have.

Billy and Simon came splashing through the puddles, snickering like they'd just won the lottery.

"We've found out what to do with beer cans," Billy
yelled.

"Yeah, my mom told us about it," Simon said. "She
told us about these guys who made a boat out of
15,000 beer cans . . ."

". . . and sailed it," Billy cut in, "from Australia
to Singapore."

"No joke. They called it the *Can-Tiki*. We figure
we could build one."

"We could make it out of 15,001 cans and get in
The Guinness Book of World Records."

"And we could call it the *CANnibal* . . ."

"Or the *CANoe* . . ."

"And sail it to *Canada* . . ."

"Up the *can*al . . ."

"I can't stand it," I yelled. "Enough, enough."

"Can we belong to your can club?" Simon asked.

"Well, why not." I was going to have to watch those guys. I really was.

At least twenty kids showed up. They were telling each other about their conies and flip-tops, deciding whether they wanted to trade a Dixie Light for a Velvet Glove Malt and wondering whether a kid's Burgermeister eleven-ounce was really worth five-to-one. Well, it wasn't winning, but it was something.

I got them all together, told them where I lived, and asked them to come to the gazebo next Saturday at two o'clock for our first meeting. "We'll make lists of the cans we want to trade," I told them, "and we can clean up the parks and get more cans and go searching in the lake on hot days. It'll be a great club.

"Now all you guys bring lists of your cans Saturday, doubles and all," I was saying, when Suzanna came whizzing round the corner on her unicycle. "Congratulations again," I called to her. "I knew you'd win."

"Thanks," she said. "You were great, Harvey. Don't go away. My dad wants to see you."

I was in for it. I just knew it. Suzanna's dad had read that article in the paper. He was going to tell me what a dumb kid I was for spouting off about how I was the greatest when I wasn't. My dad had already told me that. "You've got to stop bragging, Harvey," he said. "One, you can't go around saying you're the best at something unless you really are. Two, even if you are the best, you shouldn't say so yourself. Three, you ought to know that a batch of beer cans can't make you a king. Beer cans are just beer cans."

So I was all ready for Suzanna's dad to give me Father Lecture Number Two when he came jogging around the corner. Suzanna leaned her unicycle against a parking meter and brought him over to me.

"This is Harvey Trumble, Dad," she said.

Mr. Brooks looked me over. "So this is the Beer Can King," he said.

"Oh, no, sir," I told him. "I really didn't mean to say all that about being great and terrific. I honestly didn't know until after I talked to the reporter that you and Suzanna have a lot more cans than I do." I hoped he would just say, OK, kid, that's all right, but don't let it happen again.

"Well, Suzanna, she's the one. She keeps me out there turning up cans. It gets to you, though, like peanuts. You just can't stop searching. So, Harvey, *our* collection . . ." I tried to close my ears off so the lecture wouldn't come through so strong. "Our collection is bigger than yours," he went on, and I thought maybe he'd even start listing his biggies. "But yours just might be better."

I didn't know what he was talking about. He'd never even seen my cans. And neither had Suzanna. Then I remembered the conies we'd given her. I figured he must have thought they were doubles from my collection. Some fantastic doubles those would have been.

"Oh, you mean those conies," I said. "We gave those to Suzanna. They weren't doubles or anything, though. I'm glad you like them. They're pretty rich."

Simon heard the talk about conies and sidled up to listen.

"I figure you for a pretty smart kid, Harvey," Mr. Brooks told me. "And smart kids don't give good conies away—even to girls who are hotshots on the unicycle." He smiled over at Suzanna like he thought she was really great. "Look, Suze and I'll drop them by your house tonight—if you and your folks are going to be home."

"And *we'll* pick them up in the morning," Simon said to me. "If Billy and me are going to belong to this club, we're going to start out with first-rate cans. You want that bag of doubles back?"

"They're yours," I said, "all of them. So long as you promise not to try sailing the Atlantic in them."

Mr. Brooks reached in his jacket and took out the newspaper with our pictures on the front page. "It isn't those conies at all, Harvey. First thing I saw in the paper—after Suzanna on her unicycle—was this Hirshvogel quart conie," he said, pointing to the can I was holding in the picture. Then he laughed. "You really don't know about that Hirshvogel, do you?"

"The Hirshvogel?" I asked him. Maybe I had been wrong to tell Mr. Grundle that Mr. Brooks knew so

much. He didn't know what he was talking about.
"There's nothing to know about the Hirshvogel. It's
nothing. I've never even seen it in a beer-can book.
It isn't worth anything."

"Mind my asking where you found it?"

"It was kind of weird, really," I told him. "It was
over at the car graveyard where they've got all those
old wrecks. You know, Steve's Body Shop out on
Route 13?" He nodded. The place is a big eyesore,
my dad says, but it's been there for years on the out-
skirts of town. "Dad was looking for a fender out
there last summer and I went with him. I found the
Hirshvogel in the glove compartment of a really
broken-down old Ford. I found a flashlight, too, but
it didn't work."

"Harvey, I guess you're not going to believe this.
But you did it. You really did. Let me just tell you
about that Hirshvogel," Mr. Brooks said. "A couple
of years ago, my friend Al Bolan and me, we were at
a beer-can collectors' convention. We met this old
fellow, name of Heinrich Hirshvogel, used to own a
very small brewery in a very small Wisconsin town,
he said. He'd closed the place in the forties, during
the Second World War. He just gave it up and moved
to Chicago to live with his brother's family."

The kids had all gathered round to listen to Mr.
Brooks. I still wasn't sure what it was adding up to,
but at least I knew he wasn't mad at me.

"The old man," he went on, "came to the convention hoping to locate one of his cans. He hadn't kept

121

any. Imagine that. I guess hardly anybody kept cans in those days just for the sake of collecting them. Besides, it wasn't much of a brewery, so there weren't all that many cans in the first place. But Hirshvogel wanted one in the worst way. Just to have as a keepsake. Nobody had one. None of those collectors had even heard of Hirshvogel. The poor guy went around shaking hands and saying, 'Don't you know where I can find one of my lost Hirshvogel cans?' But nobody knew."

"You mean," I asked him, "that nobody's found one yet? The one I have is all there is?"

"I was right that you're smart," Mr. Brooks said, smiling very big. "That's about it. The beer-can magazine I get has an ad every once in a while asking if somebody's found one. People are always after things they can't have. They don't even have a photograph, just a sketch that the old man made of a blue-and-white can—steel, he said—with a gold bird above the word *Hirshvogel* on one side and a golden deer on the other."

"That's what it looks like, all right," I admitted. "But I don't think it's any big deal. It doesn't look *that* old."

"Ah," he went on, waving the newspaper in the air. "That's the thing about old cans—those made in the late thirties and very early forties. The thing about them is that they were made of heavy steel and covered with good thick labels. They were made to *last*. You see, Harvey, an old can sometimes looks a lot newer than a new one."

"But why isn't it in any of the books, Dad?" Suzanna asked, taking the newspaper from him and looking at it closely. All the other kids gathered round the paper.

Tom Andrews wandered over with a snow cone and looked at the picture. "That's nothing," he said, shrugging his shoulders. "I've seen one like that before." Mr. Brooks looked over at him, amazed. "Well, sort of like that," he said, and moved around behind a tall kid.

"Maybe it wasn't listed because nobody knows how much it's worth," Mr. Brooks said. "Soon as I saw that picture of you and the Hirshvogel this morning, Harvey, I went down to the newspaper office to get a better look. I told them about the can. Hope you don't mind. Anyway, right from the newspaper I called this man who's a big collector in Kenosha. He said if that can's the real thing, he'll give you five hundred dollars for it."

"Five hundred dollars!" I yelped. This guy is crazy, I thought. What else could I think? "There isn't a beer can anywhere worth five hundred dollars."

"Probably not." He laughed. "But I know somebody who's offered to pay you that. Personally, I'd hold onto it. You might get a better offer."

Peter came racing up on his bike. "Hey, Harvey, that reporter, Karen Gray, has been trying to reach

you on the phone. Mom said I should try to find you."
He rode over to me and joined the gang who'd been
listening to Mr. Brooks. "She told Mom that some
other papers were going to print that picture of you
and the beer can. She says one of your cans is worth
a lot of money. She told Mom you're famous."

I choked and somebody had to hit me on the back
to help me get my breath.

"You didn't believe me, did you, Harvey?" Mr.
Brooks laughed.

"Is my brother a millionaire or something?" Peter
asked.

"He must feel like one," Mr. Brooks said.

"But, Dad," Suzanna asked, "what about Mr.
Hirshvogel? Won't he want the can?" I'd been wondering the same thing.

"No," he said. "The old man died last year on a
trip to Germany. But I'll bet he would have been
plenty pleased that Harvey here found one of his
cans."

"Grab on, Harvey, I'll pull you home," Peter said,
tossing me the tow rope we keep tied to the bike seat.
"Mom's probably still talking to that reporter, trying
to find out what's going on."

I got on my skateboard and grabbed the rope, feeling as if somebody had beaned me on the head with
a baseball. "Thanks a lot, Mr. Brooks," I said. "I
might have thrown that Hirshvogel away, or something."

"Glad to be the one to tell you," he said. "But I

sure want to see it firsthand. Suze and I'll stop by this evening."

As we rode off, Peter said, "Hey, Harvey, I'm sorry you didn't win the contest."

"It doesn't matter," I told him. "It really doesn't matter."

The phone rang the minute I got inside the house. "That's Karen Gray," my mother said. "She keeps calling. I hope she's not playing a joke on you because of that egg she got hit with."

Mom was right. It was Karen Gray. She was telling me the same stuff Mr. Brooks had told me about the Hirshvogel being so rare when my dad came rushing in the front door.

"Harvey, is it true?" he asked. "Somebody just came in the store and told me you'd been offered five hundred dollars for a beer can!"

I told Karen Gray to hold on for a minute. "Sure, it's true," I told him. "I'm talking to a reporter about it right now."

"Listen, Harvey," he said quick, like it was really urgent, "I found this can on the way home." He held up a shiny new Old Chicago. "What do you think?" he asked me. "Shall we keep it?"

"Sure," I told him. "You never can tell what it's gonna be worth in a couple of years." I could hardly wait for him to meet Mr. Brooks.

"Hey, thanks for calling," I told Karen Gray. "I've got to go now."

"No, wait," she said. "I haven't come to the best

part. I really called to tell you that the wire service picked up your picture and the five hundred-dollar can story."

"Wire service?" I asked her.

"It's a service for newspapers," she said. "They send pictures all over the world, pictures of people in the news. Today, that's you, Harvey. You're news."

All over the world? Maybe the President of the United States would see my picture. Maybe the Emperor of Japan. Maybe the Queen of England would pick up her morning paper and there I'd be on the front page. "What's it look like?" I asked her.

"Well, it's that picture of you wearing your crown, holding out the can of Hirshvogel. And under it there's a paragraph about you with a heading you're really going to like."

"What's it say?" I asked.

"It says," she told me, "Harvey, the Beer Can King."

"Harvey, the Beer Can King," printed in newspapers all over the world. Harvey, the Beer Can King!

On the Fourth of July I bet they'll let me have my own float in the parade. Gold with rainbows. I'll sit on a huge throne on top and I'll wave at everybody lined up and down Lake Street. They have floats for queens all the time. Beauty queens, that's nothing. Harvey, the Beer Can King, now that's really worth a float. And once it's dark, there'll be fireworks like always. Only this year there's got to be a fireworks crown. They'll light it from the bottom and it'll slowly catch fire, fizz, and sparkle until the whole crown is flashing gold and silver. Then, POW! all at once, the words on top of it will explode in a blaze of gold. I could see it. In fireworks, *Harvey, the Beer Can King*.

"Harvey! Harvey, are you there? Are you OK?" Karen Gray was saying.

"Sure, I'm OK," I said. "I sure am." And I hung up. I could feel myself grinning.

Penalty Shot

Penalty Shot

Little, Brown and Company

Boston　New York　Toronto　London

To Brad, Mame, Tyler, and Jeremy

First Edition

Library of Congress Cataloging-in-Publication Data
Christopher, Matt.
  Penalty shot / by Matt Christopher. — 1st ed.
      p.   cm.
  Summary: Jeff, already worried about losing his place on the hockey team because of low grades, suddenly finds himself the victim of sabotage in the form of forged papers.
  ISBN 0-316-13787-1 (hc). —ISBN 0-316-14190-9 (pbk.)
  [1. Hockey — Fiction.   2. Mystery and detective stories.]
I. Title.
PZ7.M43159Pe   1997
[Fic] — dc20   96-9741

10 9 8 7 6 5 4 3 2 1

MV-NY

Published simultaneously in Canada by Little, Brown & Company
(Canada) Limited

Printed in the United States of America

ACX-9911

Penalty Shot

1

Oof!

He recovers from a block by a burly defenseman.

He's in the clear.

The puck is coming his way.

He positions his hockey stick and traps it.

Slap. Tap. Tap.

He lines it up.

For a split second, there's a clearing between him and the goal.

The goalie reaches high.

He shoots low.

Smack!

The puck careens across the ice.

It shoots by the goalie and hits the back of the cage.

Goal!

★　　★　　★

Jeff Connors raised his arms in victory. His breath came out in a fog in the crisp winter air. It was his second imaginary goal so far and he wasn't even halfway to the rink. If he could do as well when he actually got on the ice, he'd be a shoo-in to make the hockey team.

He'd made the team the year before, no problem. It hadn't been his playing ability that had kept him out of uniform. No, everyone, even the coach, had been sorry he'd been sidelined.

Jeff was willing to take some of the blame for what had happened. But he hadn't had much sympathy from the one person who could have kept him on the ice. And how was he supposed to feel about that?

Just thinking about Mr. Pearson made him angry all over again. Even now he could hear the tired tone in his English teacher's voice. "Well, Mr. Connors," he had said, "it seems you chose not to heed my last warning. I told you the consequences would be grave if you didn't. Much as I hated to do it, I fear you left me with no choice but to send a

2

full report of your current grades to your coach."

Jeff still felt as though he'd swallowed a lump of hot coal when he remembered the conversation he'd had with his coach later that day.

"Mr. Pearson tells me you knew your grades were slipping," Coach Wallace had said, shaking his head, "but that you didn't do anything about it. At least, not that he could see. Well, rules are rules. And the number one rule of this school's sports program is that if your grades fall behind, then you're off the team. I'm sorry, Jeff, but you'll have to turn in your uniform."

So that afternoon, while all his teammates were lacing up their skates and joking around in the locker room, Jeff had quietly emptied his locker. He had pretended not to notice how the room fell silent as one by one his friends realized what he was doing. The one-mile walk home that day had felt like twenty.

Jeff shook his head. That was then and this is now, he thought. Mom, Dad, and the coach are willing to give me another chance. And I'm doing okay this year.

He tried not to think about the English composition he'd put off writing yesterday. Or the spelling and reading comprehension test he'd taken two days before. If he didn't do well on them . . .

2

Jeff put all thoughts of tests and compositions out of his head. Instead, he continued his make-believe game. As he bobbed and weaved down the street, stick in ready position and his gear bag balanced over his shoulder, he was in a world of his own.

The puck curled around the boards behind the net and slid free of the tangle of players nearby. It was getting closer. He just had to dodge this one defenseman and it was his. With a quick lateral move and a jab of his stick —

"Grrrrrrr . . ."

The sound of a deep, low growl brought Jeff back to reality. He wasn't on the ice facing a defenseman. He was on the sidewalk of a tree-lined street, facing the biggest, meanest-looking dog he'd ever seen!

Jeff sprang back. The dog eyed him, baring its fangs, but didn't move.

As a five-year-old, Jeff had been bitten by a dog. He'd been nervous around dogs ever since. He usually avoided them so that people wouldn't notice. That way, he didn't have to explain anything to anyone.

Jeff hiked up his duffel bag and was about to move away when he heard a familiar voice call his name.

"Hey, Jeff, you're not going to leave without me, are you?"

It was his friend Kevin Leach. Jeff realized he was standing right in front of the Leaches' house.

Kevin hurried out the front door, stick in hand. At the same time, the dog spun around and charged. Jeff watched in horror as it jumped up at Kevin's face. He was powerless to do anything to help his friend!

To his amazement, Kevin broke out laughing and shoved the dog aside.

"So I see you've met Ranger," he said, grinning from ear to ear. "Ranger, this is Jeff. Jeff's my oldest buddy, so I want you two to get on real well, okay, boy?"

As if he understood, Ranger turned his massive head toward Jeff. Jeff took a step back.

"When did you get a dog?" he asked.

"My dad surprised me last night," said Kevin. "Some guy at his office moved and couldn't take Ranger with him, so Dad brought him home. As soon as Ranger saw me, he came right over and started licking my hand. That did it."

"I'll bet," Jeff said uneasily. He couldn't imagine anyone liking a dog licking their hand. To have those teeth so close . . .

"Luckily, Mom likes him, too. I'll feed him and walk him before school, but she's going to take him for walks during the day and when I'm at hockey practice. If I make the team, that is."

"You'll make it," Jeff said, happy to change the subject. Although they were the same age, Kevin wasn't built as sturdily as Jeff. In fact, there were times he looked downright skinny. But he was a good defenseman and he loved hockey almost as much as Jeff. "You just have to do as well as you did last year and you'll be on the team again. Hopefully, I'll be there with you."

"You'd be a shoo-in for right wing if you hadn't

been thrown off —" Kevin stopped abruptly. He shot Jeff an apologetic look. "Sorry," he mumbled.

Jeff's ears burned. "Yeah, well, that was last year. I'm not going to get thrown off the team this year. So you'd better be ready to back me up on the ice again!" He punched Kevin in the shoulder.

"*Grrrrr . . .*"

Jeff jumped back. Kevin laid a hand on Ranger's head and told the dog to shush. Then he looked curiously at Jeff. "He's a really relaxed dog, but he's been taught to protect his owner. Sometimes he gets spooked by sudden movements. He doesn't bite or anything. So you don't have to be scared of him, Jeff."

"Oh, I wasn't," Jeff said.

Kevin cocked an eyebrow at him. "Jeff, I know you don't like dogs, remember? But Ranger is different. You'll see that, once you get to know him."

Just then, Mrs. Leach opened the door. "You boys are going to be late if you don't get going," she called. "Ranger, come here!"

As Ranger bounded inside, Jeff and Kevin gathered up their gear and headed off to the rink. Kevin talked on and on about how great it was to have a dog. Though Jeff barely listened to the words, he heard one thing loud and clear: if Kevin had his way, he and Ranger would be inseparable. And if Jeff couldn't get over his fear, what would that do to their friendship?

3

Jeff pushed that thought out of his mind. He needed to get focused on what was ahead — the last day of hockey tryouts.

"I'll give you five-to-one odds," he said to Kevin as they hurried toward the skating rink.

"On what?"

"On you making the team."

Kevin grinned. "Okay, but if I'm five to one, you must be two to one. Coach Wallace has had you in the starting string practically all week. You're on the squad, no question."

"Don't I wish. You know who's a sure bet, don't you?"

The boys looked at each other and in the same breath said, "Bucky Ledbetter!"

"Talk about skating," Kevin added.

"Yeah, he's good, all right," agreed Jeff. "I just wish he wouldn't let everyone know it all the time."

Kevin shook his head. "He's loud and cocky, that's for sure. I wouldn't want to get on his bad side. He'd be one tough enemy."

"Aw, he's not so tough," said Jeff. "I tell you, though, if he ever said to me the things he says to his brother, I don't know what I'd do."

"Hayes? Boy, there's a guy who's having a tough time on the ice!"

Jeff nodded. "Bucky's mouthing at him probably doesn't help. It's funny, I heard the coach say Hayes'd be a decent player if he'd just concentrate more. I bet that's why he didn't make the team last year."

They mounted the steps to the rink. As they headed for the locker room, Kevin said, "Guess all that really matters is that we get the chance to show the coach what a dynamic duo we are together. You at right wing with me right behind you. Right?"

"Right!"

The locker room was already crowded with boys lacing up their skates and pulling on their pads. Jeff and Kevin hurried to join them. In no time at all, they were on the ice.

Coach Wallace blew his whistle.

"Okay, guys, this is it," the coach announced.

"The last day of tryouts. I'm not going to bore you with the usual speech about how I wish I could put all of you on the team, even though that's the truth." A few of the boys muttered and others hung their heads. "What you should know, however, is that I've decided to try something new this year." The same boys perked up again. "I'm going to keep two promising players on as alternates. They'll practice with the team and come to the games, though they'll only play if nobody else on the team can. This may sound like a lousy position to take. But consider how much stronger you'll be next year, going into tryouts with a whole season of practices under your belt. And here's something else to think about: if for any reason I feel there's someone on the team who's slacking off, I won't hesitate to substitute one of the alternates in his place. Now get out there and warm up!"

As Jeff took to the ice, he knew his face was beet red. A few guys glanced his way, then quickly dropped their eyes. Jeff was sure everyone there was thinking the same thing: this year, if he got kicked off the team, he wouldn't be missed. Someone else would be more than happy to step in. And more than ready.

4

After ten minutes of warm-up, Coach Wallace whistled the players back in line. He had them count off as either "in" or "out," then told the two groups to form circles at center ice.

"Here's the drill," he said. "I'm going to start the puck toward one of you. I want you to stop it, then pass it on to someone else. Don't skate after it. Just keep it moving. If you have to skate, if you miss the puck, or if you slip and fall, drop out and head for the sideline."

Coach Wallace gave a puck to the "out" group, then joined the "ins." He dropped the puck in front of himself and shot it to Shep Fredrickson. Shep stopped it carefully. He glanced around the ring and eased a pass to Michael Gillis. It slid right up to Michael's stick.

14

This looks like a breeze, Jeff thought as he watched Michael pass to Bucky Ledbetter.

Still, he remained alert, his stick in ready position.

It was a good thing he did. Bucky flipped a fast but accurate pass to Chad Galbraith, but Chad was caught napping. Coach Wallace motioned to him to skate aside. Bucky retrieved the puck and fired a lightning-quick shot right at Jeff.

Jeff reacted instantly. He stopped the puck with just enough give to keep it from bouncing back into the middle of the ring. He sent a controlled pass across to Hayes.

After that, the competitive juices began to flow as each player tried to outsmart his opponents. One player after another had to leave the circle. Soon, there were only four players left: Bucky Ledbetter, Shep Fredrickson, Michael Gillis, and Jeff.

Bucky had just received a pass from Shep when Coach Wallace blew his whistle. Jeff glanced over at the coach, ready to learn about the next drill.

Wham!

Out of nowhere came a pass so hard and powerful it almost knocked the stick from his hands. As the puck skittered away, Jeff looked back to the circle in disbelief. Bucky was grinning at him.

"Sure you're ready for this, Connors?" Bucky asked snidely. "A season away from the squad seems to have dulled your reactions."

Jeff had opened his mouth to reply when the coach called for him to retrieve the puck. With a last backward glance, Jeff skated down the ice, scooped up the disk, and hurried back to hear what the coach was telling the other players.

"Okay, same two groups," he said. "Outs, you split in half again, eight to a goal. Choose six guys to rotate in as defensemen, one player at a time. The remaining two guys will take turns playing goalie. Got it?"

The outs nodded and skated off.

"Ins, form three lines at mid-ice at the right-wing, center, and left-wing spots. Half face one goal, half the other. Your job is to get by the defenseman and take a shot on goal if you can. Easy does it on the goalie, okay? I don't want any injuries. After your run down the ice, skate back and get ready to attack the opposite goal. Got it?"

The ins nodded and scrambled to form their lines. In less than a minute, the drill started.

Jeff's heart raced with excitement. Sometimes practice could be dull, but drills like this really gave players a chance to shine.

His group was up first. Jeff was in the right-wing slot. When he saw that Bucky was in center, his enthusiasm flagged a bit. Then he shook his head, reminding himself that he and Bucky might be on the line together on the team. He had to start working well with him, just in case.

Coach Wallace blew his whistle, signaling them to begin the drill. Bucky's brother, Hayes, was at left wing. He took a pass from Bucky, then tried to shoot the puck across the ice to Jeff.

It didn't make it. Kevin skated in and stole it.

Bucky groaned. "Good move, little brother, real good move! Why don't you just pass it to the other team next time and save us all the trouble of trying to set up a play?"

He skated to the sidelines in disgust. Jeff followed him.

"Hey, Bucky, lighten up! We all send bad passes, you know," he said.

"Hayes can take the criticism. He knows I want him to get a fair crack at a place on the team this year. Unlike *last* year, when he was beaten out by someone who couldn't stick it out." Bucky cast a sidelong glance at Jeff that spoke volumes.

Jeff reddened. Darn that Bucky! He makes it sound as if I got kicked off the team on purpose!

But he swallowed his anger and skated back in line. For the rest of the afternoon he concentrated on playing as hard as he could. As a result, he made few mistakes and left practice feeling that he had given it his best shot. Now it was up to the coach to decide if Jeff was worth giving a second chance. Jeff knew he'd have his answer in less than twenty-four hours. Coach Wallace would post the team roster for all to see sometime the next day.

5

"Hi, Mom!" Jeff called out from the mudroom next to the kitchen. "Anybody home?"

"Mom's at the dentist," came a voice from upstairs. "There're some killer brownies she just made on the counter. Oh, yeah, and there's a letter for you. She put it on your bed."

"Thanks, Candy," he called back to his sister. Candy was a few years older than he was. Her life revolved around her friends in high school. Still, they had a warm relationship most of the time.

As he hung up his coat and walked into the kitchen, he wondered about the letter. He had just taken a bite out of one of the brownies when he realized who it must be from. He raced up the stairs two at a time.

There on his pillow lay a big envelope. The

return address read "The National Hockey League" along with a team name and address in red-and-blue letters. With a yelp, Jeff tore it open. A glossy black-and-white photo fell out. It was a picture of his favorite player, Eric Stone! Jeff had written to the team's fan club more than a month ago. He had started to think his letter had been lost. But here was the photo, signed and everything!

Jeff propped the picture up on his desk and was about to crumple up the envelope when a piece of paper fell out. He picked it up and stared at it, not believing what he saw. It was a letter, written to him by Eric Stone himself!

Jeff sat on the bed and read it.

Dear Jeff,

Thank you for your letter telling me how much you enjoy watching me play my favorite game — hockey. It makes it all the more exciting for me knowing that there are fans like you out there rooting for me and my team. I hope I'll live up to your expectations this season and not do anything to let you down.

Being a good hockey player takes a lot of practice. Since you say that you might want to be a professional hockey player, too, let me give you a little hint. It's not just how well you skate and handle a stick. No, you have to be a smart player, too, to get ahead in this game. That means you need a good education. That's the best way to train your mind to learn everything you have to know as a pro.

So work hard out there on the ice, but work just as hard in the classroom. Remember: keep your grades up and your stick down!

> *All the best,*
> *Eric Stone*

As Jeff read through the letter, he felt his excitement drain away. "Keep your grades up!" "Train your mind!" It was as if Eric Stone knew Jeff had had trouble in school before.

Then he began to wonder: had there been some mistakes in the letter he'd written to Eric? Maybe a misspelled word or a grammar problem? It hadn't been a very long letter but, still, he knew it was likely it had been riddled with "sentence faults" and "paragraph faults," as his teacher called them.

Why didn't I ask Candy to look over the letter before I sent it? He groaned inwardly. But he knew why. He would have felt like a little kid just learning to write. He hated feeling stupid.

Jeff took one last look at Eric Stone's letter, then crumpled it slowly in his hand. A quick toss and it was headed for the wastebasket — just as Candy walked into the room. The letter bounced off her knee and to the floor.

"Whoa, I'm unarmed!" Candy joked. She scooped up the wad and was about to toss it back at him. Then she stopped and smoothed out the paper. "Isn't this the NHL emblem? Are they writing to you to say you've been selected as the number one draft pick?"

"Very funny," said Jeff, trying to act as though it were nothing. "Here, give it to me."

But Candy was already reading the letter. Jeff turned his back on her and picked up one of his schoolbooks.

After a moment, Candy said, "I don't get it. Eric

Stone is your big hero, isn't he? So how come you're throwing away a letter from him? That's better than an autograph on a program, even."

Jeff spun around and replied, "Yeah, you're right. I wasn't thinking. Maybe I will keep it after all."

Candy held it out to him but before she let go, she asked quietly, "Are you upset about what he said about the importance of doing well in school?"

Jeff snatched the paper out of her hand and stalked over to the desk, not answering her question.

"Because if you are, I'm sure you could do better with a little extra help. Mom and Dad said they'd get you a student tutor if —"

"I don't need a tutor! I'm not stupid!" Jeff said angrily. "I just need a little peace and quiet so I can get to work on my composition. It's due tomorrow and I don't want to spend all night on it." He tore a fresh sheet of paper out of his three-ring binder and sat at his desk.

"I didn't say you were stupid," Candy said as she left the room. "At least, I don't think you're stupid in the way *you* think I mean." She slammed the door behind her.

Jeff stared at the photo of Eric Stone for a few minutes. Then, with a sigh, he turned the picture over, picked up his pencil, and tried to remember everything the teacher had told the class about writing a composition.

The clock on his wall ticked loudly. Downstairs, he heard his mother come in the back door. A truck drove by the window. Eventually, he heard his father's car turn into the driveway. Soon it would be time for supper.

The paper was still blank when he pushed himself back from the desk and headed downstairs.

Oh, well, he thought. I'll give it another try later. After I eat.

6

Is the roster up yet?" Kevin asked breathlessly as he hurried into school Friday morning. Jeff yawned widely before answering. He had stayed up late the night before finishing his composition.

"Not yet," he replied. The rink was next to the school and he had just had time to stop by on his way to school. But the list hadn't been tacked to the door. Now they would have to get permission at lunch recess to check again.

Morning classes dragged by. At lunch, Jeff sat with Kevin and a few other hockey players, but he was too nervous to eat more than a sandwich and a banana. He wasn't the only one. When the bell signaled the half hour of after-lunch free time, everyone at the table jumped up as if they'd been stuck with pins.

"I'll get the okay from Ms. Collins," Jeff said as he headed over to the teacher on duty.

Ms. Collins agreed that they could take a quick walk to the rink to see if the roster was up. As he moved to rejoin the others, Jeff heard her call out to him.

"I'll see you in English class, Jeff. I'm looking forward to reading your composition."

In the excitement, Jeff had almost forgotten about it. Well, he'd stayed up half the night working on it, so no one could accuse him of not trying. Still, as he gave Ms. Collins a half wave to show he'd heard her, he felt a knot tighten in his stomach.

No time for that now, he thought. He sprinted to catch up with the rest of the boys. Together they hurried to the rink.

The list was there! Jeff pushed his way forward and scanned it for his name. At first he didn't see it. Then he read through the roster again — and there it was! He let out a sigh of relief.

Kevin, Bucky, and Hayes had all made the squad, too. So had most of the other players from the year before. There were a few new names, too, including two way down at the bottom under the heading of "Alternates." At the very bottom of the page was a note telling players there would be no practice that day but that they should stop in and get their uniforms.

Jeff ran down the steps and searched for Kevin. He spotted him with Bucky, Hayes, and a fourth fellow he didn't recognize.

"Hey there, fellow Blades!" he called. Kevin was all smiles as Jeff clapped him on the back.

"Hey yourself," he replied. "We were just talking about getting in a little weekend practice down at the pond. Interested?"

"Sure, sounds good," said Jeff. He glanced curiously at the new person.

Kevin introduced the two to each other. "Jeff Connors, this is Sam Metcalf. He just moved here. He's going to be the team manager!"

Jeff shook Sam's hand. "That name sounds familiar," he said.

Sam shrugged. "If you read the local district sports pages, you might have seen it in a few columns about hockey last year. I led my old team in scoring. I had hoped I'd be able to play here, too. But I missed the tryouts for the Blades because we were moving."

Jeff shook his head sympathetically. "That's rough," he said. He was going to ask Sam some more questions but was cut off by the bell.

As the boys headed back to school, they settled on a time to meet for a pick-up game on the pond on Saturday.

"I'll be there," Jeff promised. "But now I have to turn in my English composition." He groaned.

"Something the matter?" Sam asked.

"Jeff has trouble writing," Hayes cut in before Jeff had a chance to speak.

Sam shot Jeff a sideways glance but didn't say anything.

Jeff reddened. "Yeah, well Hayes is so good at it he thinks anyone who doesn't get all A's has a problem. He's lucky."

Hayes smiled at him and nodded. "You're right. I am lucky."

Jeff was the last one to arrive in class. He turned in his composition and began to struggle to keep his mind from wandering. He liked Ms. Collins and really did want to do well in her class. But the afternoon sun was slanting through the tall classroom windows. Jeff found himself staring at the dust whirling in the sunbeam and day-dreaming.

I sure hope it doesn't snow, he thought. It'll be easier to play on the pond tomorrow if we don't have to clear the ice. I wonder if I'll be able to get the same number on my uniform that I had last year?

At last, the bell rang. As Jeff hurried out of the room, he could feel Ms. Collins's eyes on his back. But she didn't call for him to stay.

The final two classes breezed by quickly. Jeff grabbed the books he needed for his weekend homework, threw on his coat, and ran over to the rink. With all the other newly appointed Blades, he stood in line to receive his uniform.

"Welcome back to the team," Coach Wallace said as he handed him a bright yellow jersey with a 19 on the back. Sam Metcalf noted the number in the book he was holding, then handed the book to Jeff for his signature. As Jeff was signing, Coach Wallace added, "I hope I'll see that number on the ice the whole season this year, not folded away like last year."

"Yes, sir!" Jeff answered with an enthusiastic nod. "You can count on it!"

I hope, he added silently. He gathered up his uniform and moved aside for the next in line. I sure do hope so.

7

Saturday dawned bright, crisp, and clear. Jeff jumped out of bed, dressed quickly, and pounded down the stairs to the mudroom. He was throwing equipment into his duffel when Candy wandered in.

"I wondered what that racket was!" she said with a yawn.

Jeff answered, "I'm meeting the guys for a game, but we have to get there early before someone else gets the best spot!"

"Well, eat something first," his mother called out as he barged into the kitchen. Obediently, he wolfed down a bowl of cereal before heading out the door.

Ten minutes later he met up with the rest of the guys at the pond. It was still early in the day. With a little luck, they'd have a good couple of hours before the pond filled up with skaters. The only damper on his enjoyment was Ranger. Kevin had tied the big dog to a tree, but even so, Jeff was on the ice — and away from the dog — before any one else.

They all took time to warm up, but before long Bucky called them together to choose teams. There were six boys in all, which meant they could go three-on-three. Bucky selected Hayes and Shep. Jeff, Kevin, and Chad made up the other side.

Since they didn't have an extra guy to drop the puck for a face-off, they threw fingers to see who would be on offense first. Bucky's side won. As they skated into position, Jeff, Kevin, and Chad called out for their men.

"I've got Shep!" Kevin said. Chad yelled that Hayes was his. That left Bucky for Jeff.

"Remember, no rough stuff!" Kevin reminded them as Bucky's team started down the ice. "We don't want any injuries before the season even starts!"

The trick with playing three-on-three without a goalie was to keep the offense from getting a clear shot. Anticipating a pass, stealing the puck off a stick, and crowding your player out of position were the keys to getting the puck headed the other way.

Bucky brought the puck down the ice with control. But Jeff stuck with him, looking for any opportunity to snag the disk away from him. Bucky was forced to make a pass; Hayes missed it completely. With a crow of victory, Chad snapped it up and skated furiously down the ice undefended. He drew up short right in front of the goal and casually slid the puck between the stakes.

"Hayes! Why didn't you chase him?" Bucky yelled.

Hayes poked his stick at the ice. "I knew I couldn't catch him," he said lamely.

Bucky shook his head angrily. "You always have to *try*. If you give up too easily, the other team will *always* beat you."

Though Jeff agreed that Hayes should have tried harder, he didn't like the way Bucky was talking to his younger brother. He had started to tell Bucky to cool off when Chad skated up with the puck.

"Care to try again?" he said with a devilish

grin and a wag of his eyebrows. Everyone broke up laughing, even Bucky.

"Be prepared," was all Bucky said as he took the disk.

Bucky started with the puck again. This time, he skated in long strides to the very edge of the ice, then spun around and passed to the middle, where Shep was waiting. Kevin was caught off guard and couldn't cover his man. Shep controlled the puck easily and streaked toward the goal. Jeff made a split-second decision. He left Bucky wide open and went after Shep, yelling, "Switch!" to indicate that Kevin should get on Bucky.

But Bucky was too quick. The minute Jeff stopped covering him, he skated furiously toward the goal. Too late, Jeff realized what was about to happen. Shep glanced up, found his teammate, and slapped a pass to him seconds before Jeff reached him. It was pinpoint accurate. All Bucky had to do was deflect the puck into the goal to tie the score.

"That good enough for you?" Bucky challenged Chad with a smile.

Chad shrugged. "If I'd been involved in the play, I'm guessing I'd be taking the puck down the ice solo again. But I'm sure Jeff and Kevin did all they could." He sighed dramatically while his teammates rolled their eyes.

The two teams traded goals and good-humored jibes for another hour. Only when Bucky criticized Hayes for not playing aggressively enough did the friendly atmosphere dissolve. It was after one such comment that Jeff called for a break.

The hungry boys crowded onto the bench and shared the snacks they'd brought.

"So where do you think Coach will put each of us this year?" Chad asked around a mouthful of crackers.

"I'll probably be at center again," Bucky said.

"I'd like to be at wing," Hayes piped in.

"Ha! If you keep playing the way you've been playing today, the only place you'll be is on the bench!" Bucky snorted.

Jeff couldn't believe that Bucky had said something so mean to Hayes right in front of them. He half wished Hayes would tell Bucky off, but Hayes was silent. The other boys were suddenly busy with their laces or rummaging in their duffels for more snacks.

Kevin stood up and wiped the crumbs from his coat. "I'm going to let Ranger run around for a while, okay?" he said as he undid the leash.

Before Jeff had a chance to protest, Ranger wriggled free of Kevin's grasp and bounded over to the bench. He nosed each boy in turn, looking for a treat. They all patted him and pushed him away. When he reached Jeff, Jeff dropped the cookie he was holding as if it had burned his fingers. Ranger snapped it up and gulped it down in one bite.

Licking his chops and panting, he took a hopeful step toward Jeff.

Jeff shrank back into the bench.

"Jeff, what's wrong? You're not afraid of the dog, are you?" Chad asked.

Kevin collared Ranger and tugged him away from Jeff.

" 'Course I'm not afraid," Jeff said, embarrassed. "I just didn't like the smell of his breath, that's all."

Chad nodded his head seriously. "Must have been the cookie Shep's mom made. That was the last thing Ranger ate!"

All the guys laughed, but Jeff caught a look exchanged between Bucky and Hayes. The look seemed to say that neither boy believed it had been bad breath that had made Jeff jump.

8

By the time they had reassembled on the ice, several other skaters had joined them. Mothers with children just trying out skates for the first time, solo skaters doing fancy moves, and another group of hockey players vied for position on the small space.

"Hey, isn't that Sam Metcalf over there?" said Bucky, pointing to the second hockey group.

Kevin shaded his eyes and nodded. "You wanna see if they'd be up for getting a real game going? Looks like they have about six players, too."

"Good idea." Bucky skated off.

While they waited, Shep, Kevin, and Chad passed the puck back and forth. Jeff decided to let Hayes know he didn't approve of what Bucky had said earlier.

"Hey, Hayes," he began.

Hayes held up his hand. "Listen, I know what you're going to say. But don't worry about me. Before tryouts began, I asked my brother to keep me on my toes this year. Even though he's kind of a jerk about it, he's just trying to help me be a better player."

"But you're on the team already," Jeff persisted. "So why do you need him to keep razzing you like that?"

Hayes gave Jeff a lopsided grin. "You may have forgotten about those two alternates, but I haven't. I may be on the team now, but that's no guarantee I'll stay on it." Jeff was about to give Hayes a word of encouragement when the other hockey team skated up. As they started introducing themselves to the others, Hayes added one last comment.

"I would have thought you out of anybody would understand I don't want to be yanked from the roster. You know, since you have experience with that."

Jeff wanted the pond to open up and swallow him. Instead, a gloved hand grasped his and shook it.

Sam Metcalf was grinning at him. "Did you hear

the news?" he said excitedly. "I'm officially an alternate for the team now! One of the guys who was chosen decided he would play for an intramural squad instead, so Coach Wallace promoted me from manager to player."

Jeff smiled warmly. "That's great!" he said, liking Sam's enthusiasm. In fact, he decided he liked Sam, period. It was a feeling that grew through the afternoon as the two teams battled for the puck. Sam was a good player, confident in his own abilities but generous with his praise for his teammates. By the time the sun was setting, Jeff found himself wishing Sam had been promoted to full player instead of just alternate.

But in order for that to happen, one of the existing players would have to go. Much as he liked Sam, Jeff didn't want that to happen.

9

Two days later, Jeff found himself wishing he were back on the ice. The minute he walked into English class Monday afternoon, he knew something was wrong.

"Jeff, could I see you for a minute?" Ms. Collins asked quietly. She handed him the composition he'd written the week before. It was covered with green correction marks — and a big, fat "E."

Jeff waited for his teacher to lecture him. But she didn't. Instead, she handed him a slip of paper. "This is the name of a tutor. You have a choice: work with her to improve and this grade stays out of the book. Or, continue as you've been doing. I can promise if you choose that option, though, that you'll wish you hadn't." She softened her tone slightly. "Jeff, I'm not insisting that you get all A's instantly. Just show me that you're *trying*. You can start by doing another composition under the instruction of your tutor."

Jeff unfolded the piece of paper and read the name. Beth Ledbetter. Below there was a phone number and an address. Jeff recognized them both.

Oh, great, Jeff thought to himself. This is Bucky's and Hayes's sister! Wonder how long it will take before word gets around the team and people start taking bets on whether I'll be thrown off again or not?

Out loud, he said, "Thanks, Ms. Collins. I'll — I'll call her right when I get home tonight. Right after hockey practice, I mean."

Ms. Collins smiled at him wearily. "Of course. But Jeff, keep in mind that sometimes good grades are more important than sports. You have to learn to train your mind as well as your body. I'll look forward to seeing a different, improved composition from you in two weeks. Okay, take your seat."

For the rest of class, Jeff tried to concentrate on what he was doing instead of on the call he had promised to make. But he kept drifting back to it and to what Ms. Collins had said before she told him to sit down.

Train your mind . . . where had he heard that before?

Midway through math class it dawned on him. Eric Stone had said the same thing in his letter. Jeff knew it was time to listen to what they were saying, but he couldn't help wishing it didn't mean getting tutored by his teammates' sister! He sighed.

"Yes, Mr. Connors? Are you experiencing some hardship? Perhaps you'd like to share it with the rest of the class?" his math teacher asked drily.

Jeff shook his head. No way! he thought, as he turned his attention back to the problem on the board. I'd like anything *but* that!

At practice that afternoon, Jeff suited up right away and was one of the first players out on the ice. He skated around for a few seconds, just to get the feel of it, then came back to the bench when the coach blew his whistle.

After fifteen minutes of drills, Coach Wallace handed out red pinneys to half the players. Jeff was one of them. As he tied his pinney over his jersey, he listened to the coach explain that they were going to scrimmage for the rest of the practice. He wanted to see how certain combinations of players worked together.

Jeff lined up at right wing. Bucky took up position at center, with Hayes to his left. Looking over his shoulder, Jeff saw that Kevin was backing him up at right defense. Shep was at left defense. It took Jeff a moment to realize that the figure in the goal covered in pads and protective gear was Michael Gillis.

This could be the starting lineup, Jeff suddenly thought. His heart pounded. If I do well in this scrimmage, maybe I'll earn a permanent spot here.

Six other boys took up position on the other half of the ice. Jeff looked up to see Chad facing him.

"Are you ready to go down?" Chad whispered in his best menacing voice.

"You first," Jeff growled back. They grinned at each other and waited for the scrimmage to begin.

Coach Wallace dropped the puck for the face-off. The red team took control. Jeff circled around until he reached the right zone. He caught Bucky's eye. Bucky's stick flashed and a moment later the puck hit Jeff's stick. Without looking down at it, he checked around him to see where his teammates were. Was anyone in the clear?

Hayes was. Jeff skated forward to close the space between them a bit more, then shot him a pass. Hayes fumbled it for a moment, then gained control. But that brief delay gave his defender enough time to close in.

Jeff could see Hayes was in trouble. He wanted to help out, but Chad was stuck on him like flypaper. Bucky shook free of his defender and Hayes sent him the puck. Bucky took it behind the net, quickly shifting the play to the opposite side of the ice.

Jeff was too far in the middle to receive a pass. But Kevin was clear. Bucky passed the puck to him, then skated nearer to the goal. Jeff saw Kevin glance at him, then at Bucky. To Jeff's disappointment, he returned the puck to Bucky. Bucky scooped it up and delivered a lightning-quick backhand shot. The goalie never saw it coming. Score!

As the teams skated back into position, Kevin said to Jeff, "I wanted to give you a chance, but that big lug Chad was barreling down on you from behind. I didn't think you saw him."

"I didn't!" replied Jeff. He took up his position opposite Chad. "But I will next time."

Chad waggled his eyebrows. "We'll see about that."

At the next face-off, the blue team made a strong effort to get the draw. It didn't do much good. The puck caught an edge and bounced crazily all over the ice. Every time a player came near it, the disk went off in another direction.

Finally, the blue team got the puck under its control. The center started to move in closer to the red goal.

"Pass it!" Coach Wallace yelled. "Move it around!"

The blue center hesitated for a moment. That was his mistake. Bucky swooped in and captured the puck. Hayes was already streaking over the center line and heading for the attacking zone.

But Bucky had been stopped in the defending zone by a double team of defensemen. He couldn't pass to Hayes without risking an offside call. Even though it was only a scrimmage, Jeff knew Bucky

45

was too good a player to deliberately cause an offense. So, instead of sending the puck to his brother, he dropped a quick pass back to Shep.

Shep skated furiously into the neutral zone. By that time, Hayes had turned around and come back toward center ice. The two were close enough now for Shep to make a good pass.

Hayes collected the puck carefully and took off down the ice again. Bucky shook free of his defender and skated parallel to him. All Hayes had to do was pass the puck over and Bucky would have an easy shot at the goal.

From where Jeff was, it looked simple enough.

But somehow Hayes botched it. He sent the puck skyrocketing behind the net and around the board to the opposite side.

A blue defender pounced on it and sent it skimming down the ice. As the red team chased after it, Jeff heard Bucky hiss at Hayes, "Dummy!"

From the number of players who cast looks in that direction, Jeff knew that everyone else on the ice had heard it, too. Hayes turned bright red under his helmet but kept his eyes straight ahead.

For the rest of the scrimmage, Jeff could see that

Hayes's heart wasn't in the game. Midway through, Coach Wallace made some team changes. He brought in some guys from the bench, switched blue players to red and vice versa, and pointed the leftovers to the sidelines. Chad took over for Hayes, Bucky stayed in center, and Kevin remained where he was. Jeff wound up on the bench next to Hayes.

When the shuffling around was finished, Jeff got a surprise when he saw who had replaced him. It was Sam Metcalf!

Guess Coach really meant what he said about alternates getting even playing time, Jeff thought.

He could tell right from the first face-off that Sam was a solid team player. He, Chad, and Bucky made a powerful front line. Passes were sharp and accurate. Run after run down the ice, the threesome eluded their defenders to take shots on goal.

Fifteen minutes later, Coach Wallace mixed things up again. Jeff returned to right wing, but on the blue team, with Shep backing him up on defense. They performed well together, but Jeff still felt he and Kevin were the obvious duo.

Coach Wallace blew his whistle.

"Okay, one last change around, then we'll all cool down and head for the showers." When he had finished repositioning people, Jeff found himself on the bench sitting between Sam and Bucky. Hayes and Kevin were on the seats behind them.

"Boy, that felt great!" Sam said enthusiastically. Then his grin faded. "I gotta tell you guys, it's pretty hard sitting on the bench. I was a regular starter at my old school." He sighed.

Bucky shrugged. "Well, you never know. The reason Coach made those alternate positions is so he can dump some dead weight if he needs to — or if he *has* to. Right, Jeff?" He elbowed Jeff sharply in the ribs.

Jeff cut Bucky an angry look. "Or maybe he'll decide he wants to put a real team player, a guy who shows a good attitude toward his teammates, on the ice instead of some loudmouth who spends half his time criticizing other players!" he shot back.

"Well, I'm sure he'd rather have a loudmouth than a 'fraidy cat! Or should I say 'fraidy *dog?*" Bucky replied sarcastically.

48

Jeff felt his face turn beet red.

"Hey, you guys, break it up," Kevin whispered. "The coach is coming over."

The last scrimmage had ended and Coach Wallace was signaling the boys to skate a few laps, then head for the showers. As they made their way to the locker room, Jeff caught Hayes's arm.

"Listen, I just want you to know I thought you played well out there today."

Hayes stared at him. "What makes you think I don't think I did?" he asked.

"Come on, Hayes, I heard what Bucky said to you —"

"Will you quit worrying about me? I can handle Bucky. What I can't handle is some no-brain like you trying to mother me!"

He shook free of Jeff's grasp and ran into the locker room, leaving Jeff to stare after him in stunned silence.

10

Hayes's words were still ringing in Jeff's ears at dinner. It made what he had to do after dessert that much more difficult. But he knew he couldn't avoid it, no matter what.

So after he had helped clear the dishes, he grabbed the cordless phone and shut himself in the bathroom. He fished the slip of paper Ms. Collins had given him out of his pocket and dialed the number.

"Hello?" a female voice answered.

"Uh, hi, is Beth there?" Jeff asked.

"This is Beth."

"Oh. My name is Jeff Connors. Um, Ms. Collins said you might tutor me in English." He told her about his conversation with his teacher.

"Do you still have the composition you turned in?" Beth asked.

"Sure," he replied.

"Good," she said. "Sometimes people get so angry they tear them up. So we're off on the right foot already."

She sounded so nice that Jeff started to relax. Maybe this tutoring won't be so bad after all, he thought. If only it wasn't Bucky's and Hayes's sister!

"Bring your composition with you tomorrow and we'll get started," Beth said.

Jeff gulped. "So soon?" he asked. "I have hockey practice tomorrow, then I'll want to eat dinner. Couldn't we start this weekend? And couldn't you come over here?"

"No, I'm sorry, but I'm all set up here. And it really would be better to get you going sooner rather than later. It will only be for an hour. So how about it?"

Jeff sighed, knowing she was right. "Let me check with my folks, okay?" He got permission from both his mother and father, then told Beth he'd be at her house at 7:30 sharp.

I only hope the Ledbetter brothers aren't around, he thought dismally. But what are the chances of that?

School flew by the next day. Jeff told Ms. Collins he was going to be seeing Beth that very night. She looked so pleased that he was glad he hadn't put off his first tutoring session.

At practice, he concentrated on playing well. He was rewarded by being teamed up with other players he knew would be selected for the first string. Happily, Kevin was in the defenseman slot behind him more often than not.

When the session was over, Coach Wallace announced that they would be playing a non-league game on Saturday afternoon. The starting lineup would be posted Friday before practice.

Whose names would appear on that list was all any of the guys could talk about. Heated discussions about who had seen the most playing time during practice, who played well with whom, and why certain combinations of front line and defense made the most sense took up all the conversation in the locker room.

"Listen, there's no way he's going to put Shep Fredrickson and Jordan Owens together on defense," argued Chad. "They both play the left side of the ice better than the right! One's going to be a starter, the other will sub in."

Shep said, "Kevin, you and Jeff make a good front line/defenseman team. I'll bet you guys start out on the right wing and defense slots."

Only Michael Gillis seemed sure of his place on the team. He was a safe bet for the starting goalie slot and everyone knew it.

Though he listened carefully, Jeff didn't take part in the conversation. He was too busy wondering what his first tutoring session was going to be like.

Jeff and Kevin walked home together as usual, but for some reason Jeff didn't feel like telling Kevin what he was doing later that night.

He'll find out soon enough, he thought ruefully. If Bucky sees me, I'm sure he'll let the whole team know.

At dinner, Jeff ate as if he'd never seen food before, then gathered together everything he thought he might need for his meeting: his three-ring binder, his composition, a pencil, and a pen. His mother drove him to the Ledbetters' house, promising to be back in an hour. She handed him an envelope with Beth's name on the outside and a check on the inside, then drove away.

Jeff walked to the front door and rang the bell. Hayes answered it.

"Jeff! What're you doing here?" Hayes asked, looking surprised.

"Uh, I'm here to see your sister," Jeff mumbled.

Hayes stepped aside. "Come on in," he said.

"Is that Jeff Connors?" a voice called out.

Blushing furiously, Jeff pushed past Hayes just as Beth came into the room. While they shook hands, Hayes muttered something about going to his room and disappeared.

Jeff liked Beth immediately. About the same age as his sister Candy, she was dressed in sweats and running shoes. Her blond hair was cut short and her blue eyes were sizing him up just as he was sizing her up.

"Come on into my study," she said. "And let's see what you've brought me."

"Oh, uh, here," Jeff said, fumbling with the envelope his mother had given him.

Beth laughed. "I meant let's take a look at your composition, but since you're offering . . ." She whisked the envelope out of his hand and stowed it quickly in the top drawer of her desk.

"Now let me see the famous composition, the one with all the green marks," she said with a smile.

"Oh, boy, here we go," said Jeff.

"Don't worry," said Beth. "Believe me, the worst part is just getting here, and that's over and done with."

Jeff looked at her with raised eyebrows. "How'd you know that?" he asked.

"Hey, I was once in your shoes myself," she said. "Everyone goes through a slow patch in school. Only some of us get down to a crawl and need a little help to get back on track. I'm here to do that for you."

She read through the composition. Then she pulled out an expensive-looking binder. She flipped it open to a blank page and jotted down some notes.

"Okay, here's what I see you doing wrong," she said matter-of-factly. "You write incomplete sentences, for one thing. You know, missing a verb or a noun or something important like that. You also switch tenses in mid-sentence and mid-paragraph. You'll be talking in past tense one minute, then suddenly we're in present tense! Without the right tense, your work won't make sense."

"You're a poet and don't know it?" Jeff asked with a smile, referring to her little rhyme.

"Believe it or not, it's things like that that will help you remember what to watch for. I'll teach you a whole ton of stupid sayings like that, and you'll never be able to get them out of your head. Like that old '*i* before *e* except after *c*' one."

Jeff grinned. "I see what you mean. So, what else is wrong?"

Beth listed a few other problems she'd noticed. When she was through, Jeff felt a little overwhelmed and told her so.

Beth punched him lightly on the arm. "Hey, you don't have to tackle it all at once. That's why I'm here — to help make things clear."

Jeff tried to keep a straight face but burst out laughing. "Is becoming a poet part of the bargain?"

Beth laughed with him, then said, "Just keep that attitude and you'll be writing sonnets in no time. Now let's get to work."

11

The remainder of Jeff's week was filled with classes, practices, and tutoring sessions. His meetings with Beth were getting a little easier, though the first time he ran into Bucky, he was embarrassed. Bucky had razzed him about the tutoring until Beth told him to lay off. Since then, Bucky had given him a nasty smile but said nothing.

Despite this, Jeff fell into bed each night tired but satisfied that he was doing everything he could to stay on track in school and in hockey.

When classes let out on Friday, the members of the Winston Blades hockey team raced to the rink. As promised, the roster was posted. It read this way:

Center — B. Ledbetter

Right Wing — J. Connors
Left Wing — C. Galbraith
Right Defense — K. Leach
Left Defense — S. Fredrickson
Goal — M. Gillis

Jeff and Kevin slapped each other a high five, then hurried to change for practice. On the way, Kevin whispered, "I'm glad the coach finally decided to pair Chad up with Shep at left wing and left defense. Chad and I worked okay together at right when you were on the bench — better than Hayes and Shep did at left! — but I think Chad and Shep are a real power team, don't you?"

Jeff nodded. "I was a little worried yesterday that Coach was going to play Hayes at right instead of me."

Kevin shrugged. "Nah, you and I are too good together. Besides, I'm sure Coach'll sub him in, just like he does during practice. He likes to play everybody during these non-league games. Gives him a chance to see who might crack under pressure!"

As they wrestled into their gear and laced up their skates, one last thought occurred to Jeff. "Do you think Coach'll sub in the alternates tomorrow, too? I'd sure like to see how Sam Metcalf does during a game."

"Better be careful what you wish for, pal. If Sam comes in, you may find yourself warming the bench!" Kevin teased.

Jeff laughed. "Good point! Forget I said anything!"

The two skated onto the ice for the warm-up. Before the practice began, Coach Wallace gathered the team together for a pep talk. "Okay, Blades, listen up! Today we practice long and hard. Tonight you sleep long and hard. Tomorrow you eat a good breakfast and lunch and show up here raring to go! I'll want to see fire in your eyes, sparks flying from your skates, and every player looking sharp and ready! Be here by two so we can get in a warm-up before the game starts. Any questions?"

A loud chorus of no's rang across the rink.

"Well then, what are you waiting for?" Coach Wallace roared. "Get on that ice and give me three lines!"

The boys clambered on and took their positions. Jeff could see that everyone was gung ho to do his best. He felt pride in his team and in himself for being a part of it.

Best of all, it didn't seem as though any of the others had heard of his tutoring sessions.

Guess Bucky decided not to say anything, he thought. And that's just fine with me!

12

Bright and early Saturday morning, Jeff checked his duffel bag to make sure he had all his hockey equipment. He had an appointment with Beth and planned to go to the game immediately afterward.

It had been Beth's suggestion that he try writing his make-up composition before the game. "That way, when you win, you'll be able to celebrate instead of having to do this assignment," she said. It made sense to Jeff, so, after a hearty breakfast of pancakes and sausage, he hurried over to the Ledbetter house, ready to get the job done before he headed for the rink.

Beth showed him into the study. Jeff reached into his duffel for his notebook, then slapped his hand to his head.

"I forgot to bring paper!" he moaned. Beth laughed.

"What kind of tutor would I be if I didn't have paper?" she asked. She pulled out her binder and opened it. Jeff noticed again how expensive it looked. Beth caught his look.

"My dad got it for me," she explained, showing him her initials embossed on the front. "All three of us Ledbetter kids have one."

Jeff saw for the first time that the binder was a two-ring. Beth pulled the rings apart and handed him some notebook paper. She told him to start writing his make-up composition and said that she would check on him in half an hour.

Left to himself, Jeff's mind went blank. He just couldn't think of a thing to write. Instead, he fiddled with the big rings on his notebook. He pulled them open and snapped them shut, open and shut.

This is ridiculous, he thought. Coming up with a subject should be the easy part, right?

Yeah, right.

He got up and shook out his arms and legs. He could see heavy gray clouds drifting by the study window. As he stared out, he saw Kevin come down the street leading Ranger on a long leash. The black dog frolicked about, barking and sniffing everything in sight. Kevin grinned at Ranger and ruffled his fur.

That's it! Jeff suddenly thought. I'll write about Kevin and Ranger!

He made it through the first paragraph. Then he ran out of things to say. After sitting for five minutes, staring at the half-empty paper, he suddenly thought of a better topic. He tossed the first sheet into the trash can and started again.

This time, he wrote about Eric Stone's letter and how it had helped him decide to try working with a tutor.

When Beth knocked softly on the door, he was ready.

Beth settled herself in an armchair. "So, what did you decide to write about?" she asked.

"Well, I started writing about my friend Kevin and his dog, Ranger. I'm not a big fan of dogs, but I want to try to like this one since it belongs to my best friend. But I didn't get very far, so I decided to write about my favorite hockey player and a letter I got from him."

Just then, the doorbell rang. Beth moved to

answer it, but before she had risen from the chair, Bucky walked by the study door.

"You guys keep working, I'll get that," he said.

Beth looked startled, then puzzled. "I thought he was up in his room," she said. "Oh, well, he must have been on his way to the kitchen or something. Anyway, mind if I take a look at the paper?"

Jeff handed it over. "You've written a lot there," she observed. "Now let's see how you've done."

Beth's usual way of correcting his papers was to circle his errors in red. Then they worked together to figure out how to correct them.

But when she handed him back his paper this time, he saw there were only red check marks in the margins on the side of the paper.

"I've indicated the lines where the errors are," she explained. "Now it's up to you to find them and fix them."

"But I'm the one who made the mistakes in the first place!" Jeff said. "How do I find them?"

"You've been training yourself all week to construct sentences that make sense. Be a detective and sniff out the clues!"

Jeff focused his attention on the sheet of the

paper and stared at the first check mark. Then his eyes slid across the line to the sentence. After a moment, his eyes lit up.

"I see it!" he said triumphantly. Before long, he had found the rest of the mistakes as well. He and Beth talked them over and she agreed that he had identified them all.

"Now all that's left is for you to copy the composition over on a clean sheet of paper and hand it in on Monday," Beth said with a smile.

Jeff nodded. He was still nervous about his writing, but he accepted a fresh piece of paper from her special binder. Slowly, carefully, he rewrote the composition. When he was done, Beth pronounced it perfect. "But I don't think you have time to listen to my praises. Don't you have to be somewhere?"

Jeff looked at the clock. It was 1:40! "Yikes! I'm supposed to be at warm-ups in twenty minutes!" He gathered up the two papers, shoved them into his duffel bag, and ran for the door. Just before he left, he called out, "Thanks, Beth!"

She grinned and replied, "Just make sure that paper gets to Ms. Collins in one piece!"

13

Jeff ran all the way to the rink. He was panting like a dog on a hot afternoon when he burst into the locker room.

"Whoa, where's the fire?" Kevin asked jokingly.

"I lost track of time!" Jeff said, gasping for breath. A moment later, Hayes Ledbetter came hurrying in.

"Hayes! I thought you'd come over with Bucky. I would have waited for you," Jeff said.

"That's okay," Hayes said. "Bucky came early. I had some things I had to do. Guess I lost track of time."

"Sure sign of a real professional," a voice behind them said. It was Bucky. "What were you doing, playing computer games?"

"It was a — an extra-credit writing exercise,"

66

Hayes mumbled. Bucky rolled his eyes and snorted.

Jeff felt sorry for Hayes and wished his brother would lay off him for one minute. But he didn't say anything because he knew it was none of his business.

He headed for the ice the minute he was suited up. Several other players, including members of the other team, were already warming up. Jeff waved hello to Chad, Shep, and Sam, then concentrated on preparing himself for the game. When the whistle blew, he was raring to go.

Coach Wallace called them all together. "Okay, Blades, this may not be for the record, but think of how great you'll feel to have a real win under your belts! So go out there and do your stuff!"

The boys cheered. The starting lineup took their positions. Jeff glanced back at Kevin, who gave him an excited thumbs-up.

Bucky and the center for the Clover Rovers readied themselves for the face-off. When the referee dropped the puck, they scrambled frantically. Bucky came out the winner.

He slammed a pass to Chad almost immediately.

Chad controlled it and headed down the ice. A defenseman was on him like glue. With a swift flick of the wrist, Chad passed the puck back to Bucky.

Jeff followed the action closely, looking for a chance to help out. When Bucky received the pass, Jeff faked out his defenseman and skated free.

"C'mon, Bucky, give it up! I'm in the clear!" he muttered to himself. As if he had heard him, Bucky sent the puck skimming over the ice toward his right wing.

Jeff reached the puck, but a second later he was slammed into the boards by an out-of-control Rover defenseman. No foul was called. With a grunt, he pushed himself off. The puck skittered away from him. But to his relief, he saw Kevin snatch it up.

Kevin skated slowly toward the middle, apparently looking to pass to either Bucky or Chad. But Jeff knew better. Kevin was preparing for a play they had perfected in the past week. All the Blades knew what was coming, but Jeff counted on the Rovers being fooled.

They were. When Kevin turned quickly and passed the puck to Jeff, Jeff was practically standing by himself. He skated with fast, slashing moves right toward the goal. But at the last second, he slipped behind the net and ricocheted the puck against the boards.

Chad was already on his way to meet it. Like a well-oiled machine, his stick found the puck. All he had to do was backhand it into the goal. And that's just what he did.

Cheers roared up from the Blades' bench and the few fans who had come out to watch the non-league event. Jeff beamed, knowing that the scorekeeper was putting a nice fat check mark down in the assist column beside his name.

Back at center ice, Bucky and the Rover center were ready for the next face-off. This time, the Rover won. He made a beeline pass to his right wing. The wing treated it like a hot potato, wasting no time in sending it right on back.

Shep was too quick for him, however. He sneaked in and stole the puck in mid-pass. One swift move later and Chad had control. But not for long — he tapped the puck just a little too hard and sent it skimming beyond his reach. A Rover defenseman picked it up and gave it a hearty whack.

It had all happened so quickly, the rest of the Rovers were caught off guard. The puck whizzed by them despite their desperate lunges to stop it. Kevin nabbed it and moved behind the Blades' net. When he emerged on the opposite side, Shep was waiting. Kevin passed off, and Shep kept the puck going, this time sending it to Bucky.

Bucky stickhandled the disk straight down the center of the ice. As Jeff skated to stay parallel with him, he knew his efforts were wasted. Bucky was going to drive in and shoot the puck right down the goalie's throat if he could.

He could. Bucky pulled up short with an ice-flying stop and, with a move so quick it was difficult to follow, launched the puck into the air. It soared past the goalie's outstretched glove and into the net for the second goal of the game.

Coach Wallace took advantage of the break in action to put in some subs. Chad and Jeff both came out, as did Shep. With a slight twinge of jealousy, Jeff noted that Hayes had replaced him at right wing. He told himself not to be greedy, however, and grabbed a seat next to Sam Metcalf.

Sam offered him a cup of water. Jeff drank it

gratefully. Then he watched the game and shouted encouragement with the rest of the bench.

"Sure hope I get out there sometime today," Sam said at one point.

Jeff felt sorry for him. He knew only too well what it was like to want to play. Of course, Sam stood a very good chance of seeing ice time — unlike Jeff the year before.

Well, that's not going to happen this year, not with that composition I've got sitting in my duffel bag, he thought with determination.

Sam did get a chance to play later in the game. Coach put him in at right wing after he took Hayes out. Sam impressed everybody on the team with his sharp passes, speedy skating, and aggressive play. He even assisted on the Blades' third goal of the day.

"Looks like you and I are neck and neck for assists!" he commented when Jeff came in to replace him. Jeff grinned back.

"We'll see if I can't change that!" he called.

But three goals were all the Blades would score that game. It was enough to give them the win. And as Coach Wallace had predicted, even though it wasn't for the record, it felt good.

The mood in the locker room was jubilant. Jeff and some of the other boys even sang victory songs while they showered.

Towel around his waist and still singing, Jeff left the shower area to get dressed. When he turned the corner to his row of lockers, he stopped abruptly. His locker was wide open and a figure was crouched in front of it. Jeff could see that the person's hand was on the zipper of his duffel bag.

"Hey!" Jeff yelped.

The figure spun around. It was Sam Metcalf!

"What are you doing?" Jeff asked, his surprise clearly showing on his face.

Sam looked puzzled. "What do you mean? I'm getting my stuff together!"

"You're getting *my* stuff together, you mean," Jeff corrected him. "That's my locker and my duffel bag!"

Sam let go of the duffel as if it were on fire. Then he peered up at the number on the locker door.

"Number 207, whoops," he said. "I thought this was number 107." He hurried over to the next row and came back carrying a duffel. Except for the fact that the handles on Jeff's bag were gold while Sam's were white, the two bags were identical. "See why I got confused?"

Jeff laughed. "Yeah, no problem," he said. "But I think I'll count my socks just to make sure there are still two of them in here. Can't be too careful, you know!"

Sam laughed, too, then disappeared into his own row of lockers. Jeff heard him humming the victory song.

14

Jeff loafed around for the rest of the weekend, enjoying the fact that his homework was already done. When Monday morning came, he set off for school with a light heart. His composition was tucked neatly in his notebook. For once, he was looking forward to English class.

But Ms. Collins wasn't in class that day. A short, gray-haired man with wire-rimmed glasses was sitting behind her desk when Jeff arrived.

"Ms. Collins is away at a teachers' conference. I'm substituting for the week," explained the stranger.

"Oh, I have this composition to turn in," said Jeff. "Maybe I could leave it on her desk?"

"Fine," said the substitute. "I'll add a little note to document when it was turned in. Just put it down there."

Jeff did, then took his seat.

"Guess we'll soon see how good a tutor my sister is, huh?" whispered Hayes across the aisle.

Jeff nodded. He didn't want to admit it, but he was a little disappointed Ms. Collins wasn't there to read the composition right away. Then he smiled to himself.

Who would have thought I'd be anxious for someone to read something I'd written? he thought. As he listened to the substitute drone on, he found himself wishing for another reason that Ms. Collins were there — at least she made the material sound interesting!

At practice that afternoon, Coach Wallace sat the Blades down on the benches. He praised them for their solid victory against the Clover Rovers. He was pointing out some of their mistakes when the sound of a door slamming made him stop.

Jeff turned with the rest of the team to see who was causing the commotion. It was Hayes Ledbetter.

"Nice of you to join us, Hayes," the coach said sarcastically. Hayes mumbled something about being tied up with a teacher unexpectedly.

The rest of practice was uneventful. The only exciting thing that happened was Coach Wallace handing out the game schedule. Their first league game was to take place on Saturday.

Jeff and Kevin talked about the practice and the upcoming game the whole walk home. They were only interrupted when Kevin's helmet fell out of his duffel bag.

"How'd that zipper get unzipped?" Kevin wondered. "I was sure I'd closed it tight."

"Maybe it's broken," Jeff replied.

Kevin grimaced. "If it is, I'll be in big trouble. This bag is practically brand new!"

"Here, let me see it," Jeff said. He took the helmet from Kevin, shoved it into the bag, then fiddled with the zipper for a moment until it worked again. "There you go. Nothing I wouldn't do to keep you out of trouble!"

They parted laughing. Jeff hurried the rest of the way home, hungry for dinner.

He ate two helpings of spaghetti and three rolls. "No room for salad," he said when his mother urged him to eat "some kind of green thing." But he managed to polish off a bowl of ice cream ten minutes later.

"Okay, mister, time to earn your keep. Those recycling bins aren't going to wait any longer," his father said when the dishes had been cleared.

Jeff groaned, but heaved himself up. He knew it wouldn't take long to finish his chore. Then he could sack out on the couch for a while.

Mr. Connors had built a number of collection bins onto the side of the garage. Jeff's job was to separate the material for recycling and the bottles and cans to be returned to the market from the rubbish. Once a month, he joined his father on the trip to the recycling center, where they turned in all that they had collected. Jeff's father paid him ten dollars each trip, so Jeff couldn't really complain.

He had just brought out a stack of magazines that he'd tied up with a piece of string when he heard someone whistling a tune out in front of the house. He looked down the driveway and saw Kevin passing by with Ranger on his usual long leash.

Jeff watched them for a moment or two. Ranger really did seem like a well-behaved, friendly dog.

And he was on a leash. Jeff decided now was as good a time as any to try to learn to like Ranger.

"Hey, Kev, how are you and the dog doing?" he called out as he walked toward them.

Kevin's head snapped around. "A fat lot you care! You'd probably be happy if my dog dropped dead right in front of you, wouldn't you! Come on, Ranger, let's get out of here!"

Jeff was stunned. Instinctively, he ran down the driveway after them.

He was too late. The darkness of the night had swallowed them up. Before long, he couldn't even hear the sound of their footsteps. But Kevin's words continued to resound in his ear, loud and clear.

As soon as Jeff got back to the house, he picked up the telephone and called Kevin.

The line was busy.

He tried again five minutes later. This time the call went through.

"Hi, Mrs. Leach? This is Jeff. Is Kevin there?" he asked. He heard her muffle the phone and call out for Kevin. Then she got back on the line.

"Kevin's doing his homework right now, Jeff. He can't come to the phone."

"Oh," said Jeff. "Well, could you tell him . . . tell him that I called? Thanks." He hung up the phone.

I'll corner him at school tomorrow, he promised himself, and find out what the heck this is all about!

The next morning Jeff arrived at school earlier

than usual. He found his way to Kevin's locker and waited for him to show up.

Kids came by, opened their lockers, put away their coats, took out books. But no Kevin.

Wonder if he's home sick? Jeff thought.

Yet on his way to class, he spotted Kevin at the end of a long corridor. He was coming out of the administrative office.

Late, I guess, Jeff figured. He was just late, that's all.

The two boys had one class together: history. Jeff was sure Kevin wouldn't miss that. He decided to talk to him there.

But when he arrived, Kevin was up at the front of the room talking to Mr. Leone, their teacher. Jeff moved up closer, but there was no way he could interrupt their conversation. Finally, everyone but the two boys was seated.

"Whatever it is, Jeff, it'll have to wait until after class. Take your seats, please, boys," said Mr. Leone.

Frustrated, Jeff moved to his desk. Kevin's chair was across the room, so he didn't stand a chance of talking to him all period.

When the bell rang, Kevin was off like a flash.

But Jeff was in hot pursuit.

"Just a minute, Jeffrey. Wasn't there something you wanted to talk to me about?" Mr. Leone asked. Jeff slowed down long enough to say he'd figured it out on his own. But by the time he'd reached the hallway, Kevin was nowhere to be seen.

For the rest of the day, even at lunch, Kevin eluded him. It was only when they gathered for hockey practice that Jeff had his chance to confront him.

Even then, Jeff could tell it wasn't going to do any good.

"Will you just tell me if I heard you right last night?" Jeff demanded.

Kevin simply stared at the floor and shook his head. He laced on his skates furiously and stomped on his runners out of the locker room without a word.

Jeff decided the only thing he could do was wait for Kevin to talk to him. For now, he'd just go through practice as usual.

But practice was anything but usual. Every time Coach Wallace teamed Jeff and Kevin up on the right side, Jeff felt as though he were playing with someone he'd never met before.

"I'll bet you didn't connect on one pass the whole time you were out there," said Coach Wallace to the two of them when they were on the bench. "I suppose it had to happen sometime. I just hope that it's not a permanent situation. I'd hate to have to rethink my starting lineup again. But maybe I'll have to do just that."

Jeff's face didn't show it, but his heart sank. He had tried so hard to earn his place on the team. He decided then and there that he wasn't going to let some attitude of Kevin's blow it for him.

When practice was over, Jeff was all set to make a beeline for Kevin. He was going to get to the bottom of things right away!

But on the way to the locker room, Bucky grabbed his arm. Jeff struggled to shake him loose, but Bucky held him tighter. "Listen," he said. "Keep away from Kevin in there. I'll talk to you after he's gone."

Jeff looked at Bucky with surprise and nodded. Maybe Bucky knew something about it. It was worth checking out, anyway.

When the locker room had cleared out, Bucky

came over and sat next to Jeff.

"All I can tell you is that you'd better back off for a while," he said. "Kevin hasn't said much except that he's really steamed about your note."

"My note? What note?" Jeff demanded. "I don't know anything about any note. What's he talking about?"

"Search me," Bucky said with a shrug. "I'm telling you everything I know. And giving you my advice to stay away from him until he cools down."

But Jeff just couldn't leave it that way. He'd gone a whole day without speaking to his best friend. He was determined that the next day would be different.

That night after dinner, he got permission to go to Kevin's house. Instead of going around back as he usually did, he rang the front doorbell. He didn't want to give Kevin a chance to hole up.

Kevin answered the door. Ranger was right behind him, swishing his tail and barking.

"Quiet, Ranger," Kevin said. Then he looked at Jeff. "What do *you* want?"

Jeff drew a deep breath. The sight of Ranger had shaken him, but he knew he had to get by the dog in order to talk to Kevin. So, while Kevin stood with his hand on the doorknob, Jeff barged right in and headed for Kevin's room.

"Hey! Wait a minute!" Kevin called. "Ranger, come on!" He followed Jeff into his room and demanded, "What do you think you're doing?"

Jeff shut the door. "I don't want anyone to interrupt us."

Kevin hugged Ranger protectively. "If you lay one finger on my dog —"

"Why would you say something dumb like that?" Jeff asked, shocked.

"Why? Because you said yourself that if you ever got the chance, you'd see what you could do to get rid of him. Well, I'm not going to give you that chance!"

"I never said anything like that!"

"Did too! You even put it in writing!" Kevin jumped up, tore open his desk drawer, and shoved a piece of paper in Jeff's hands. "Just try to deny it now!"

Jeff unfolded the paper and read:

There may be a lot of nice dogs in this

*world, but some are just plain mean. Kevin's
dog Ranger is one of those. I don't know why
Kevin spends so much time with him since he's
such a dumb dog. In fact, he'd be better off if
he had Ranger put away so that he didn't
waste any more time on that rotten mutt.*

Though there was something slightly familiar
about it, Jeff knew he'd never written that paragraph.
He'd never written — or said — anything so awful.

Yet the handwriting looked just like his! Before
he had a chance to examine it closely, however,
Kevin had snatched it away from him.

"You're pretty quiet all of a sudden," Kevin said
accusingly.

"Kevin, I didn't —"

"I know what your handwriting looks like."

"But I never wrote that!" Jeff shouted. "Where
did it come from? Where did you find it?"

"You know I found it in my duffel bag last night.
I bet you put it there when you pretended to fix my
zipper!"

Jeff shook his head. "But Kevin, why would I
want to write something like that?"

"Who knows?" Kevin said, avoiding his eyes. "All I know is what I know. And I know that you don't like dogs and that that's your handwriting on that piece of paper. So if you didn't write it, tell me who did." He walked to his door and opened it. "If you can't tell me that, then we have nothing to say to each other."

The next day, Jeff had only one thing on his mind: to find out who had played such a dirty trick on him and his best buddy. But no matter how much he puzzled over it, he couldn't figure out who would do such a rotten thing. Or why.

He and Kevin played no better together than they had at Tuesday's practice. Jeff had never realized before what a difference good communication between teammates made. Now he felt the effects of bad communication every minute he was on the ice.

It was the same thing on Thursday. Kevin avoided him at school and didn't talk to him at all at practice. The other Blades were starting to notice. Jeff saw Sam Metcalf talking to Kevin. The two glanced over at him and Kevin shook his head.

Though he couldn't hear what they were saying, Jeff was sure they were talking about him.

By the time Friday afternoon rolled around, Jeff was sure he wasn't going to be seeing his name on the starting lineup roster.

But he was wrong. When the list went up, he saw that Coach Wallace had stayed with the same six players. He could only hope that Kevin would put aside his anger by game time Saturday.

If only I could figure out who the saboteur is! Kevin thought desperately. It seemed hopeless.

Jeff and Beth Ledbetter had continued to meet off and on throughout the week. On Friday afternoon, Beth said Jeff seemed to be getting the hang of it, but that he should still consider coming by for his Saturday morning session. Jeff agreed. Now that he knew he was still in the starting lineup, he didn't dare risk letting his grades slip!

"By the way," Beth asked. "What did Ms. Collins think of your composition?"

"She hasn't been around to read it yet," Jeff said.

"Well, I hope it's in a safe place. It'd stink if all your hard work wound up missing or damaged!"

Saturday morning, Jeff awoke to see snow falling

outside his window. He could smell scrambled eggs and English muffins cooking in the kitchen. With a contented sigh, he rolled out of bed to start his day.

Half an hour later, his mother dropped him off at the Ledbetters' house. He and Beth worked together for an hour and a half. Then it was time to get ready for his game. He had left his duffel bag in the car, so when his mother picked him up, they were set to head straight for the rink.

Jeff hopped out of the car, promising to make a goal for his mom. In the locker room, he dressed quickly, slipped on his skate guards, and hurried out to the rink.

As usual, a feeling of anticipation hit him the minute his skates touched the ice. The thrill of competition ahead always gave him a rush. He loved it all — the feel of the ice beneath him, the bright lights, the cold air on his face as he skated on the shimmering surface. He had to control his impulse to pour on the speed. He knew it would be better to save his strength for the game ahead.

And then he heard a familiar voice near the water jug.

"Are there any cups?" Kevin asked.

Within seconds, Jeff's happy mood was replaced by uneasiness. How will Kevin and I do on the ice together today? he wondered. We have to play better than we did this week.

But even as he thought it, he had a bad feeling that things weren't going to go well.

Minutes later, the rink was filled with skaters from both teams warming up. The Fremont Penguins were in solid blue with white numbers. They made a nice contrast to the Winston Blades' yellow uniforms.

Finally, the whistle blew and the two teams separated to their respective benches.

"Okay, let me have your attention," said Coach Wallace. "I want to see some heads-up hockey out there. Quick passes, sharp and accurate. Keep your eye on your positions. Talk to one another and set up the plays we've been working on all week. We're only a good team when we play like a team."

Jeff caught Kevin's eye for a brief second. Then Kevin looked away.

I hear you, Coach, Jeff thought. Hopefully, Kevin does, too.

Coach Wallace interrupted his thoughts by

yelling that it was time to take to the ice. Jeff shook his head, determined to stop puzzling over his problem until after the game. Instead, he skated onto the ice with the other Blades and prepared himself for the face-off.

The whistle blew. The puck dropped and the two centers scrambled to get their sticks around it.

The puck skittered on its edge past Jeff, rolled onto its side, and slid across the ice toward a player in blue and white. The Penguins took charge, dribbled it past the red middle line, and headed toward the Blades' goal.

The action skipped from one side of the net to the other. But the puck never went in. Kevin finally managed to grab it after two good saves by Michael Gillis.

"Kevin! Kevin!" Jeff shouted. He was near the blue line, ready for a pass.

Kevin ignored him. Instead, he passed the puck to Chad, who dribbled it across the blue line. Bucky caught a pass from Chad and brought it across the midline into goal-scoring territory.

Jeff tried to get himself into a good scoring position. He waited for a pass, hoping that Bucky would put into action a play he, Jeff, and Kevin had had good luck with in the past. Before the note, that was.

Darn that note! Jeff thought angrily. It really messed things up!

As he thought about it, he felt something hit his skate.

The puck! He had let his mind wander only for a moment, but that had been long enough for him to miss out on making the play work. He tried to control the disk, but it ricocheted off his blade and slid back to the blue line.

Luckily for the Blades, Kevin was there. He trapped it with his stick, dribbled it into position, and slammed it toward the center. Bucky was right there. He caught the puck, spun around, and hit it with a forehand shot that went streaking at the net — and in!

Goal!

The Blades cheered and waved their sticks in the air as they congratulated Bucky and Kevin. The Penguins called for a time-out.

Clustered around their own bench, the Blades gave Coach Wallace their full attention.

"That goal was deserved," he said, "but it's time to start setting up some plays out there. Keep moving that puck and then take your best shot." The referee blew the whistle. "One second, Jeff. You, too, Shep. Hayes, I want you to go in for Jeff. Jordan, you go in for Shep. Boys, grab some pine here."

Jeff's heart sank. He'd been in the game just five minutes. He took a seat behind Sam Metcalf without a word. Shep plunked down next to Sam.

Sam nudged Shep. "Hey, at least you're wearing a uniform," he said quietly. "I'd do just about anything to get on the squad. I'm likely to be sitting here all season in plain clothes unless . . ."

Jeff's ears perked up. He waited for Sam to finish his sentence. When Sam didn't, Jeff silently finished it for him.

Unless someone on the team has to give up his uniform.

17

Jeff tried to concentrate on the game. But he couldn't stop thinking about Sam. If Sam thought breaking up a good combination on the ice — a combination like Jeff and Kevin had been before the note turned up — would help his chances of getting on the team, would he try to do it?

Sitting behind Sam and listening to him cheer on the Blades, Jeff just couldn't believe he was capable of such a thing. He couldn't believe it, but couldn't deny that such a motive could have led to the note.

With a sigh, he turned his attention fully on the game.

The Penguins had taken control of the puck after the face-off. This time they weren't about to give up easily. The game got a lot more physical. First a two-minute penalty for high sticking was called on the Penguins. Then Bucky was caught elbowing an opponent. Since the penalties left both teams short a man, neither converted them into a power-play advantage.

After several more minutes of back-and-forth shots on goal with no scoring. the first period ended. Coach Wallace had Jeff go back in for Hayes, with a caution to keep his eyes open and let his teammates know his position at all times.

Jeff was rested from his time on the bench and ready to play hard. The face-off went to the Blades. Jeff worked to get free for a pass. His first thought was to set up one of the plays with Kevin that worked so well. But before he could make another move, someone crashed into him from the side.

A burly Penguin defenseman sent him reeling toward the boards. Frantically, Jeff struggled to regain his balance. But at the last minute, his skates flew out from under him and he sprawled onto the ice.

As the referee's whistle blew, Jeff felt a spray of ice in his face. A player had skidded to a stop just shy of his prone body.

"Here!" a gruff voice said. It was Kevin, holding

out a hand. "Come on! We've got just two minutes to put together a power play!"

Jeff grabbed the hand and scrambled to his feet. "Thanks," he said. But Kevin had skated off already.

For the next two minutes, the Blades tried to make the power play work. As the penalty time ticked down, it seemed they wouldn't be successful. Even though the Penguins were down a man, they had everyone covered.

Then Kevin got control. With a quick glance up, he sent the puck skimming toward Jeff. Jeff stopped it. Seeing that he was clear, he skated furiously in the direction of the Penguins' goal.

Closer. Closer. He shuffled the puck back and forth with the tip of his stick. Chad raced parallel with him down the ice. At the last possible second, Jeff flicked the disk across to the left wing. Chad simply let it ricochet off his stick toward the goal.

The Penguins goalkeeper lunged for it. But he was too late. The puck hit the back of the net — and the Blades were up 2–0!

Jeff and Chad slapped high fives and cheered. Jeff looked for Kevin to thank him for feeding him the puck. But when he caught his eye, Kevin just jerked his head up in acknowledgment and skated away.

Well, it's not much, but at least he's thawing a little, Jeff said to himself.

The Blades set up for the face-off. Jeff and the rest of the players tried their hardest to sweeten the lead. It was no use. The Penguins played by the book, sticking to their men like sand on a wet foot, stealing the puck every chance they could, and passing with finesse. By the end of the second period, they had inched up on the Blades with two goals of their own.

"You can take these guys," Coach Wallace assured them at a break. "Let's see some energy out there!"

But those two Penguin goals had dulled the Blades' sharpness. There was no spark. There was no extra push. And most noticeably, there were no words of encouragement on-ice. In fact, there was the exact opposite.

"C'mon, Chad, I'm way ahead of you!" Bucky Ledbetter yelled after his left wing passed the puck too far behind him.

"Shep, where's the backup? Where's the backup?" Chad cried when Shep failed to pick up a pass that had skimmed under Chad's stick.

"Can't see! Can't see!" Michael Gillis called frantically when a pile of players landed in a heap near the goal.

Only Jeff and Kevin were silent.

When the buzzer ended the last period, Jeff had had it. He couldn't have cared less that their first game had concluded in a tie. All he wanted to do was shower up, walk home, and sit in the peace and quiet of his bedroom.

Most of all, he wanted to stop thinking about dogs, mean notes, and friendships gone sour.

18

Two days later, a dark cloud still hung over Jeff's head. He struggled through his morning classes. At lunchtime, he sat with the rest of the hockey team but didn't say a word. When he was through eating, he mumbled something about having to go to the library at free time afterward.

This day just can't get any worse, he thought as he crouched in the racks of books, pretending to read a biography on a famous hockey player.

But it did. Ms. Collins was back in class — and she wasn't happy. She handed him his make-up composition with a shake of her head.

As soon as he looked at it, he knew why she was upset. It was covered with green correction marks. There was no way he could have received a passing grade.

She must think I didn't even try! Jeff thought dismally.

Then the full magnitude of the situation hit him. If he didn't get a passing grade, he could kiss his place on the hockey team good-bye.

His heart started thudding. Desperately, he scanned the paper again. This time, he saw something he hadn't seen before. He looked more closely to be sure he wasn't mistaken. He saw he was right.

The places he remembered correcting were wrong again. But more than that, *new errors had appeared!*

This isn't the paper I left with the substitute, he realized. It's been changed.

Yet the handwriting looked like his. How could he explain that away?

It's not the first time you've seen something in your handwriting that you knew you didn't write, a little voice inside his head said. The saboteur has struck again. Whoever wrote the note to Kevin also tampered with this paper.

But how was he supposed to convince Ms. Collins of that? And what was she supposed to do even if she did believe him? He still owed her a composition.

Suddenly, an idea struck him. It was his only chance. It would make him a little late — maybe a lot late — for practice, but there was no other possible way.

After class he tried to explain the situation to his teacher.

"Uh, Ms. Collins," he began. He told her how hard he had been working with Beth Ledbetter, how he had written the composition and given it to Beth to look over before handing it in, and how he had his suspicions that someone had messed with it while Ms. Collins had been away. "It's just not what I wrote," he finished.

"I must say I was surprised when I saw it," Ms. Collins admitted. "And disappointed. Beth Ledbetter is far too good a tutor for you to do *worse* after working with her. But Jeff," she added, "that handwriting is so much like yours. I don't know what to make of it."

Jeff cleared his throat. "Well, what if we just pretend it doesn't exist? If you can spare a little time, what if I come back here after school today and write a new composition in front of you? That way you'll be able to see for yourself how I've improved."

Ms. Collins lifted an eyebrow. "But Jeffrey, won't staying after school interfere with hockey?"

Jeff returned her grin. "As someone once told me, sometimes you have to train your mind as well as your body. So what do you say?"

"It's a deal. Be back here at two-thirty sharp."

Jeff nodded, gathered up his books, and rushed to his next class.

Well, that's one problem taken care of, he thought. That leaves two to go: getting Kevin to believe me, and finding out who's trying to do me in!

When the bell rang signaling the end of his last class, Jeff hurried back to Ms. Collins's room. As he turned a corner, he bumped right into Kevin.

Kevin frowned and started to move around him.

"Kevin, wait! I know you're still mad at me, but I really need your help." When he saw Kevin hesitate, he blundered on. "Can you tell Coach I'm going to be a little late to practice? I — I have to meet with my English teacher."

Kevin grimaced. "Your English teacher? Are you in trouble in that class again?"

"I don't know for sure. That's what I have to go find out. Please help me?"

Kevin sighed loudly. "Yeah, sure, I'll tell him. While I'm at it, should I let Sam Metcalf know his chances of suiting up next game are looking pretty good?"

"Just deliver the message to the coach, okay? And Kevin," he added, "I'm going to find out who wrote that note."

But Kevin was already walking away.

Shaking his head, Jeff hurried the rest of the way to Ms. Collins's room. While she sat at her desk correcting papers, he took a seat, pulled a fresh sheet of notebook paper out of his three-ring binder, and began to write. The clock on the wall behind his teacher's desk ticked away the minutes, one by one. But Jeff barely heard it.

He quickly filled the page, then put his pencil down.

Now I have to remember what Beth taught me. I have to go back over it and make sure that I've done everything right. *All the clues are there.*

Beth had been talking about writing when she had said that, but Jeff realized the same statement could be applied to finding his saboteur. With a smile, he set to work on ferreting out the mistakes he'd made on the paper.

He pored over his work carefully. He made some erasures, fixed spelling, and then he rewrote parts of it — until finally he was finished. Half an hour had passed.

He stood up and handed his paper to Ms. Collins. "Here it is. Every single word of it is mine."

Ms. Collins nodded. "Care to stick around while I correct it?"

Jeff sat down again. For the next few moments, he sat tensely as Ms. Collins's green marker moved above his paper. He couldn't tell how many times she used it to make a mark, but she seemed to be examining every letter with extreme care.

That's what I should be doing, Jeff thought. Only the paper I should be checking over is that phony composition. If it hadn't been for that, I'd be over at the skating rink by now!

He pulled out the green ink–filled page and

looked at it closely for a third time. And that's when he saw them.

They were faint, but they were there. Little red check marks down the side of the margin.

This wasn't the paper he had turned in. This was the first draft of the composition!

Hold on, he thought. That draft is still in my notebook, isn't it?

He whipped through his notebook quickly. He found an old science test, the start of a letter to Eric Stone, and some doodles, but no first draft.

Beads of perspiration formed on his forehead.

Slowly. Don't jump to any conclusions. Take another look.

He forced himself to be very careful as he turned each page of the notebook again.

There was no doubt about it. The paper Beth had corrected was missing. Somehow or other, it had found its way into Ms. Collins's desk.

But how?

No, not *how*, Jeff thought suddenly. *Who*. Who would have known that I had a draft of it in my notebook and why would he have swapped the two? And is it the same person who left that note for Kevin?

Suddenly, Jeff recalled the time he had found Sam squatting over his duffel bag. He had taken Sam's explanation of mistaken identity at face value then. But now he wondered. The compositions had been in his duffel that day. What if Sam had seen them, taken the draft for some reason, then tampered with it? They did play the same position, after all, and what had happened to Jeff the year before when he had failed English was common team knowledge.

I'd do just about anything to get on the squad. Isn't that what Sam had said?

His thoughts were interrupted by Ms. Collins.

"Well done, Jeffrey," she said, beaming. "This is excellent work. It shows a great deal of promise. I knew you could do it."

"Is it — is it good enough to give me a passing grade?" Jeff asked nervously.

"Definitely. As a matter of fact, what are you doing lingering here? Don't you have a practice this afternoon?"

"I sure do! Thanks, Ms. Collins! Thanks a lot!"

19

Jeff raced to the locker room and suited up in record time. He didn't bother snapping the rubber runners onto his skates, he just dashed into the rink, ready to join the others on the ice.

To his surprise, everyone was seated in the stands. Coach Wallace had obviously called for a break.

"Well, nice of you to join us," the coach said, looking at his watch.

"Didn't Kevin tell you I was going to be late?" Jeff held his breath while he waited for the answer.

"He mumbled something about your being delayed by your English teacher," said the coach. "Since you're here, I guess that means you didn't lose your eligibility."

"No, I definitely did not. Despite what certain

people may think, I am still on the team!"

A few heads turned in his direction. Jeff returned their looks straight on before shifting his gaze back to the coach.

Coach Wallace cleared his throat. "Well, glad to hear it," he said mildly. "Now then, Blades, let's run a few more drills before we break down and scrimmage."

As the boys clambered off the benches to the ice, Jeff caught up to Kevin.

"Thanks for delivering my message," he said.

Kevin shrugged.

"Listen," Jeff continued. "Do you still have that note? I'd like to take another look at it."

Kevin stared at him. "I've got it at home, as a matter of fact. Though why I haven't burned it yet, I don't know."

Jeff gave him a small smile. "Maybe it's because you were hoping I'd be able to figure out who really wrote it. You knew you shouldn't destroy the evidence!"

"Maybe," Kevin replied gruffly. "Anyway, if you really think it'll do any good, I guess you can come over to my house after dinner and see it."

Jeff gave a silent cheer. Then he turned his attention back to practice.

Coach had set them up for a passing drill. He wanted them to concentrate on giving and receiving strong, accurate passes. As always, he stressed the importance of letting the stick give at the moment of contact. A bad "catch" could send the puck off in any direction.

Jeff turned in a fine performance in both forehand and backhand passing. When the drill switched to shots on goal, he made sure his were lightning quick. The last set of drills involved dodging a defenseman while carrying the puck, then skimming a pass off to a teammate. Jeff had little trouble with that exercise, either.

But throughout the various plays, Jeff's mind strayed to other things. Like what he thought he'd find when he looked at Kevin's note again — and how he hoped it would prove beyond a doubt that he was innocent.

20

Jeff rushed through dinner that night. He excused himself as soon as he could and mumbled that he had to see Kevin about something.

"That's fine," his mother said. "I've been wondering if there was something going on between you two. I haven't seen Kevin around for a while."

"Everything is fine. Or at least, it will be," Jeff answered. Then he jammed his hat on his head, zipped up his coat, and grabbed his book bag.

Inside were his notebook, the mysterious first draft of the composition, and the one he had just written that afternoon for Ms. Collins.

When he rang Kevin's doorbell, the door opened immediately. Kevin stood there with Ranger at his side.

Jeff took a deep breath. Then he did something

he had never thought he would do. He held his hand out toward Ranger's nose.

Ranger sniffed it. Jeff slowly moved his hand from in front of Ranger's nose to the top of Ranger's head — and patted him!

Ranger's tail thumped and Kevin's eyes widened. "Well, I'll be," he said. He stepped aside to let Jeff in. "Come on up."

Kevin led the way to his bedroom. The note was lying on his desk. Jeff picked it up eagerly.

At a glance, he saw his instincts had been right. And he knew that there was no way Sam Metcalf was involved. Without a word, he set it back down on the desk and unzipped his book bag. He withdrew his notebook, opened the three rings, and took out a blank sheet of paper. Then he dug out the two compositions. Finally, he laid the note alongside them.

With a gesture of his hand, he asked Kevin to compare the four pieces of paper.

Kevin took a moment, then shrugged. "I don't get it. If I'm supposed to be comparing the handwriting, I still can't see a difference. But what's the blank page for?"

Jeff just said, "The clues are all there. Keep

looking and I think you'll see for yourself."

So Kevin looked again. And this time he saw what Jeff meant.

"This, this, and this," he said, pointing to the two compositions and the blank sheet, "are all three-hole-punched pieces of paper. But this one," he finished, picking up the note, "is a two-hole. And the ink used in the lines is a funny shade of blue. It's almost purple. The paper feels smoother, too."

Jeff nodded solemnly. "I've only seen paper like that once before."

"Where?"

"In Beth Ledbetter's notebook. Her dad gave her a special binder filled with it last year."

Kevin stared at Jeff in amazement. "You mean *Beth Ledbetter* wrote this note? I don't believe it!"

"No, not Beth," Jeff said. "But someone who has a binder just like hers. That someone had to know an awful lot in order to write that note. He had to know that Beth was tutoring me, that I had written a make-up composition, and that my topic had been about you and Ranger. And since I'm pretty sure whoever wrote that note also sabotaged my

112

make-up composition," he finished sadly, "that someone also had to know what would happen to me if I got a failing grade."

"You sound like you already know who it is," Kevin said.

"I think I do. But I'll need your help to prove it." Then he told Kevin who he thought the perpetrator was and why he had done it. Kevin whistled.

"If it's true, then he's in for some big trouble," he said.

"I know. But even though he messed things up between you and me, I wish there was some way of keeping him out of it. But he brought it on himself. No one forced him."

"So what now?"

"Now, I think we have to come up with a plan for flushing the criminal out."

The boys talked for the next hour. Then Jeff got up to leave.

"I'll see you tomorrow, Kevin. Pick you up at seven-thirty to go to school. Okay?"

"Tell you what," Kevin replied. "Come by at seven and help me walk Ranger."

Jeff grinned. "You got a deal."

21

Classes flew by the next day. When practice started, Jeff and Kevin put their plan into action. It started with a fight.

"That stupid dog of yours tipped over our garbage cans this morning," Jeff said to Kevin. He punctuated his accusation by poking a finger into Kevin's chest.

"Did not!" Kevin replied angrily. "You probably tipped them yourself just so you could blame Ranger!"

"It would serve him right if he became known as a menace to the neighborhood."

"Oh, so you admit you tipped them?"

"No! But it's probably just a matter of time before he proves what a worthless, mean mutt he is. He'll bite someone or bark his head off all night or chase people on bikes. Your flea-bitten mongrel will get what he deserves soon enough!"

Kevin spun on his heel and stomped to his locker. The other boys looked at each other uneasily.

"What's all that shouting?" Coach Wallace entered the locker room holding his clipboard. "Well?"

"Nothing, Coach," a few of the boys mumbled.

"Then what are you all lollygagging around for? Get suited up and out on the ice! Pronto!"

As Jeff headed for the door, he saw Kevin hold the door open for Hayes and Bucky. Bucky seemed to be badgering Hayes about something. Hayes just shook his head but didn't say anything.

Coach Wallace had the team set up for a scrimmage immediately after warm-up. The lineup was as usual: Chad, Bucky, and Jeff in the front, Shep and Kevin backing them up, and Michael in the cage.

The coach played referee and dropped the puck for the face-off. Bucky controlled it right away and sent it skimming to Chad. Chad skated with it for a few feet, then lateraled it back to Bucky. Bucky dodged a defenseman, glanced up, and found Jeff in the clear.

Jeff stopped the puck easily, but instead of taking off down the ice with it, he slowed his pace. His heart pounded. Okay, Kevin, he said to himself, here we go.

As if he had heard Jeff's thoughts, Kevin started skating furiously. Jeff turned a blind shoulder to him and braced himself.

Wham!

Kevin hit Jeff full force and sent him reeling. Jeff collided with the boards and fell hard. He didn't get up.

Coach Wallace blew his whistle. All action stopped as he sped over to the prone figure.

Jeff sat up, looking dazed. He stood slowly but winced as he put weight on his left foot.

"I — I think it's sprained, Coach," he said weakly.

"Kevin, help Jeff into the locker room," Coach Wallace said.

"No," Kevin said in a low voice.

Shocked, Coach Wallace stared at him. "What do you mean, *no!*"

"Not until he confesses."

The coach looked baffled. "Confesses what?

116

What's this all about?"

"Confesses that he put a bunch of mean notes threatening my dog in my locker! I've been getting one every day this week!"

"*What?*"

This time, it wasn't the coach who had spoken. It was Bucky Ledbetter.

Coach Wallace turned to him. "Do you know what's happening here, Bucky?" he asked.

Bucky swallowed hard. "I — I'm not sure. I mean, I know a little of it, but that's all."

Coach Wallace continued to look at him. Bucky dug his skate into the ice. "I should have said something sooner, but I didn't know how. And I thought it was only that one time. I didn't know it had been going on longer."

He looked up and shot a glance at his brother.

The coach caught the look. So did everyone else. Hayes stood there, his head hung low.

"It was me," he mumbled. Then he lifted his head. "But I only put one note in Kevin's locker. One! I don't know where the other ones came from."

Jeff moved forward. "There were no other ones. Kevin and I just pretended there were, hoping you'd come forward to deny it."

"And it worked," Kevin added.

Jeff nodded. "You got pretty good at my handwriting, Hayes. But how?"

"I — I found part of a composition you'd written in my sister's trash can. I traced some of it. Changed words from what you had written until it was the note Kevin got."

Bucky cut in. "I caught him doing it," he confessed. "I should have stopped him, but he told me it was just a joke. By the time I realized it wasn't, it was too late."

Jeff whistled. "I thought the note sounded so familiar. I just couldn't figure out why." He shook his head. "You might have gotten away with it, Hayes. But you forged my writing again, didn't you? By replacing my good composition with one you had tampered with?"

"Yeah." Hayes sounded defeated. "I grabbed your draft out of your notebook while you were giving the real one to the substitute. Then I just changed a few things and switched them later that week."

"Why'd you do it, Hayes? What did I ever do to you?"

Then it all came out. "You stood in my way. I didn't make the team last year because of you. Then you got thrown off and I was still sitting in the stands! Now this year, when you shouldn't have even been allowed to try out, you're playing first string."

"But you made the team this year and you're subbing in all the time!" Jeff said in amazement.

"Yeah, but how long can that continue? We all know there's a better player just waiting for me to slip up." Hayes's eyes slid over to Sam Metcalf.

Sam looked startled. "Gee, Hayes, I guess I can't deny that I'd rather be a full-time player than an alternate. But I want to earn my uniform, not get it because someone was thrown off!"

Coach Wallace put a heavy hand on Hayes's shoulder. "Hayes, I think you better go to the locker room. I'll be there in a moment. The rest of you, set up a shooting drill."

Hayes slumped, then skated slowly away. The other boys silently shuffled into place for the drill. Once it was going, Coach Wallace started toward the locker room.

Jeff broke out of his line and caught up to him.

"Coach, what are you going to do with Hayes?" he asked.

The coach shook his head. "What do you think, Jeff? I can't let him off the hook."

Jeff looked the coach in the eye. "Please don't kick him off the team," he said quietly. "Hayes made mistakes — big ones — but I can understand what made him do it. I — I know what it's like to worry about keeping your place on the team. And I'd hate for him to go through what I went through last year."

Coach Wallace studied Jeff for a moment. Then he said, "Well, since you were the person most likely to be hurt by what Hayes did, what would you suggest I do?"

"I know Hayes has to be punished. But couldn't you switch him to alternate instead of kicking him off the team altogether? He's really shaping into a good player, and if he gets a season of practices under his belt, I bet he could be a real asset to the team next year. Plus, maybe if the other guys see that you and I are willing to give him another chance, they'll forgive him, too. I know I'll never forget that you gave me another chance."

Jeff held his breath while the coach thought it over. Then he nodded. "Okay, Jeff. If Hayes is willing to move to alternate, then I'll let him stay on."

"Great!" Jeff cried. "Thanks, Coach!"

"Don't thank me. It's your plan. And I'll be sure Hayes knows it. Now get back out there. We've got a game this Saturday and I want all my players to be prepared!"

22

Saturday morning, the snow was flying thick and fast. Mr. and Mrs. Connors drove Jeff to the rink. Even Candy decided to watch the game.

The first thing Jeff noticed when he came into the locker room was that Sam Metcalf was in uniform. And that Sam looked unhappy.

"I just don't feel right, wearing this," he said to Jeff. "I didn't really earn it."

A lull in the chatter made Jeff and Sam turn. Hayes had come in and was walking straight toward them.

"You deserve to wear that more than I do," he said. "You've been practicing just as hard as any of us."

Hayes turned to Jeff. "Coach told me what you said. Thanks for giving me another chance."

"Hey, I know what it's like to feel insecure about something. For me, it's writing. And dogs, too, I guess, though I'm getting over that with help from Kevin and Ranger. For you, it was your ability to play good hockey. But both of us are improving. And don't forget, next year Bucky and the other ninth graders move on to high school, which means there will be a few more open spots on the team. Who better than you to fill one of them?"

Hayes cracked a small smile. "Yeah, good point. Well, good luck in the game. Show those Groveland Jets who's boss!"

Ten minutes later, Jeff was on the ice waiting for the referee to drop the puck for the face-off.

The whistle blew and the puck hit the ice. Bucky gained control immediately and shot the disk to Jeff. Jeff captured it and took off into the attack zone.

From behind him, Kevin called out, "I'm with you if you need me!"

Jeff spotted Chad skating neck and neck with his Jets defenseman. Then he broke free and skated quickly toward the goal. With a smooth move, Jeff sent the puck sailing to his stick.

But it was picked off before it reached Chad. The Jets defender dodged around Chad and made a move toward the Blades goal.

He hadn't reckoned on Shep, however. The powerful defenseman slipped in, stole the puck off a bad tap, and passed it cross-ice to Kevin.

Kevin protected the puck by skating close to the boards. Jeff took up position directly in front of him. With a backhand sweep, Kevin sent the puck skimming up to Jeff's waiting stick.

Jeff spotted Bucky skating alongside him. "Three!" Bucky yelled, signaling that they were in prime position to put play number three into motion. With a nod of acknowledgment, Jeff sent the puck to Bucky, then set off.

All Jeff had to do was work his way to about six feet in front of the net and a little off to the right side. Kevin would come skating by him as though he were going to take a pass from Bucky. But he'd let the puck go by him. Then Jeff would grab it, spin around, and slap one into the net. The surprise element was crucial if the play were to succeed.

Everything happened exactly as it should have.

Jeff got into position. Bucky held on to the puck. When Kevin made his move, he gave no indication that he was even aware of Jeff's presence. But in contrast to the last game, Jeff knew this was just a ruse. Kevin was playing his part perfectly.

And it worked! Kevin shot past Jeff just as Bucky let the puck fly. Jeff stopped it and a second later sent it sailing into the goal!

Sticks waving madly in the air and cheers erupting from their throats, the Blades crowded around Jeff to congratulate him. Then they quickly got into position for the next face-off.

Jeff turned his head slightly as he waited for the whistle. Out of the corner of his eye, he saw Kevin give him a thumbs-up sign.

Jeff knew that even if the Blades didn't win the game, he was going to go home happy.

When the ref took position for the drop, Jeff couldn't control himself.

"Let's go, you guys!" he yelled. "Let's show 'em who's boss!"

"Heads-up playing!" Kevin joined in.

"Dig in!" echoed Shep.

The whistle blew. The puck dropped. Bucky missed

it this time, but Shep acted quickly and intercepted a pass the Jets center tried to make to his wing. Shep skated forward a few feet and passed to Chad.

Chad took long, smooth strokes, carefully controlling his speed and the puck. It seemed as though he was taking his time, that he didn't really care if he brought the puck into scoring position or not.

But his lazy attitude was deceptive. When a Jets defenseman attacked, Chad made a sharp lateral move. The Jets player had so much forward momentum that he rocketed right into the boards behind Chad.

Chad skated calmly forward a few more feet, heading straight toward Bucky.

Jeff knew what was coming. And sure enough, no more than six feet in front of the goal, Chad and Bucky passed one another almost shoulder to shoulder. The puck slipped from Chad's stick to Bucky's. Bucky took up the left-wing position while Chad, pretending to have the puck still, stopped abruptly as if he were about to shoot.

The Jets were fooled for no more than a second. It was long enough for Bucky to sneak into position for a shot on goal. But his attempt failed when the puck ricocheted off the goalie's pads and onto the waiting Jets stick.

Back and forth the play went. By the end of the first period, the shots-on-goal statistics showed that both teams had had many chances to score. But the board still read Blades 1, Jets 0.

At the start of the second period, Coach Wallace subbed in a few players. Jeff and Bucky came out. Sam and the second-string center went in.

Bucky moved close to Hayes on the bench.

"Listen, little brother," he said. "I hope you can follow Jeff's lead and forgive me."

Hayes stared at his brother.

"For razzing you so hard the beginning of the season," Bucky continued. "I think maybe it had something to do with what you did, huh?"

Hayes shrugged. "Maybe a little," he said. "But no one can take the blame for what I did but me. And at least I'm still part of the team. Sam and Jeff just better look out next year, that's all!"

Jeff grinned at him. "I'll give you a run for your money, just you wait," he promised. "Now let's stop all this true-confessions stuff. We've got a game out there to win!"

Read them all!

All available in paperback from Little, Brown and Company